Seas
of the
Wheel

TALES, POEMS, MEDITATIONS AND VEGAN RECIPES

To Susan,

Bright Blessings

Sue x.

The wheel turns, the seasons of the year pass as fleeting memories. Once more tales, poems, meditations and vegan recipes are woven into the passing seasons.

SUE THORNE

Seasons of the Wheel

First published 2022 by Compass-Publishing UK

ISBN 978-1-913713-95-9

Copyright © Sue Thorne, 2022

A CIP catalogue record for this book is available from the British Library.

Printed and bound by The Design Hive

Cover design by © The Design Hive

FOREWORD

I hope that some of you have enjoyed reading my first book, The Ever Turning Wheel. I had planned to leave the tales of the village at that point, however several readers have asked, "What happens to Demi and her family next?" well dear reader, read on. Brightest Blessings.

The Village does exist, the main inspiration for the location is the beautiful village of Lustleigh, South Devon, however the village green and village hall I have 'stolen' from the equally beautiful village of North Bovey just a few miles from Lustleigh. The other village locations are based on the villages of Ford and Etal in Northumbria.

All of the characters in these stories are a figment of my imagination and are not based on any individual either living or dead.

For those of you who may be new to Paganism or may wish to find out more about our festivals this is the order we usually celebrate them in the Northern Hemisphere.

A Pagan year usually runs from Samhain to Samhain. Many Pagans mark the 1st November as the new year, myself included, though others prefer the Winter Solstice as a beginning and end, however as the Wheel is constantly turning there is no ending or beginning.

The dates of the festivals are as follows;

Samhain Sunset 31st October until Sunset 1st November.

Yule or Mid Winter Solstice, any time between Sunset 19th December and Sunset 22nd December, these are claimed to be the longest nights of the year.

Imbolc Sunset 31st January until Sunset 2nd February.

Ostara or Spring Equinox any time around Sunset 19th March until Sunset 23rd March, day and night of almost equal length, from now on the days begin to get longer.

Beltaine or May Day Sunset 30th April until Sunset 1st May.

Summer Solstice, any time between Sunset 20th June until Sunset 23rd June, these are the shortest nights of the year.

Lughnasadh or Lammas Sunset 31st July until Sunset 2nd August.

Mabon or Autumn Equinox any time around Sunset 19th September until Sunset 23rd September, once again day and night of roughly equal length, from now on the days begin to get shorter.

As you can see there is a festival each month, some are in the middle of the month others are spread across the cusp of two months. The festivals are roughly around six to seven weeks apart.

VEGAN RECIPES

I have included some vegan recipes appropriate to each festival at the end of each chapter. Some are recipes that I have used for many years, others I have devised for this book. I have spent a great deal of time writing out recipes and weighing out ingredients to get them just right. This is a first for me as, apart from baking, I usually throw in a little of this and a bit of that when I am cooking. Of course you can eat any of these dishes at any time of the year. If you fancy Yule (Christmas) pudding in September, well why not?

I have been careful not to include weird and wonderful ingredients, they are mostly things that you would usually have in the store cupboard or are easily obtained. I have also used the same ingredients in several recipes to cut down on food wastage. There is nothing worse than buying a specific ingredient for a dish to then leave it in the store cupboard to discover it a few years later covered in green goo. I feel I must thank the members of our pagan group who have been willing tasters and testers. Thank you.

MEDITATIONS

There are nine meditations in the book, one for each of the seasons, except for Lughnasadh where there are two. They are written in such a way that they have natural pauses when the journey takes you from one place to another, they are marked in this way ......

Most people now have access to a recording device, I suggest that you record them and then play them back when you wish to leave the hustle and bustle of daily life.

SEASONS OF THE WOODS

Holly stands ever green, his leaves shine brightly in the harsh mid-winter sun,

Red berries shimmer, they sustain blackbird and redwing,

The ever-present robin sings his lonely song, deep within the spiny tipped boughs.

Snowdrops begin to stir,

Grey/green leaves emerging between the leaf litter,

First heralds of the coming spring.

Next come primroses and violets to carpet the woodland floor,

Tips of Elder and Hawthorn tentatively test the cool early spring air,

Tiny green fingertip shoots appear.

Old man's beard is also out and about, soft green leaves brave the cold,

The Alder stands naked still, his boughs covered in cones and catkins,

It will be a while before he is brave enough to show green.

Hazel, Beech, and Silver Birch are next to bring forth shoots,

Hazel catkins sway gently in the cool spring breeze,

Soft yellow spires release pollen to drift upon the air, our noses to tickle.

Black bird, blue tit and thrush begin to swell the robin's lonely song,

A frenzy of territory forming and nest building from dawn to dusk,

Eggs laid in perfectly made nests, patiently brooded.

Now is the turn of the mighty Oak to begin to grow,

Soft coppery green leaves adorn the naked winter stems,

His stately trunk covered in soft green moss and ivy climbs towards the sky.

Bluebells, wild garlic, and unfurling ferns adorn the woodland floor,

Witch's whiskers lichen decorates almost every tree,

Branches covered in soft sage green growth.

Last, (but never least,) to appear the Ash sends forth his new spring growth,

Beautiful Ash how long will you last to herald the summer?

Without you, we and our woodlands will be the poorer.

YULE

A VILLAGE TALE

*O*ur *Village tales continue, the Wheel has turned once more from Samhain to Yule. The dark days of Winter hold the land in its grasp, the Winter Crone rules the short days and the long bitterly cold nights. Soon the celebrations of the Sun God's rebirth will help to bring cheer to this dark time of the year. The time to decorate our homes with Winter greenery, the time for sharing good food and drink and fireside tales with family and friends.*

So far it had been a bitterly cold winter, the leaves had all fallen from the trees by the end of October and the first snow had fallen by mid-November. The snow had lingered for many days before a thaw had set in. The melting snows from the high moors above swelling the stream that flowed through the Glade and orchard and then in turn down through the village. Now in mid-December the snow had fallen once again, and the village was covered in a thick, even white blanket. Demi, who was first up in answer to Oak's calls, helped her son onto the window seat to show him the almost enchanted view as the snow glittered and sparkled in the bright winter sunshine.

"Look, isn't that pretty?"

"Yes, it is very pretty," agreed Oak. He turned to look at Demi, a knowing look in his eyes. Demi smiled at her son; he was so knowing for a child of his age. "It is your birthday in a few days' time at the Winter Solstice, you will be three years old. Where has that time gone my little one?"

Demi knew only too well where the time had gone, village life revolved around the turning wheel of the year. Oak was born at the Winter Solstice just before the dawn began to break.

1

Then the wheel had turned towards Imbolc, Ostara, Beltaine, the Summer Solstice, Lughnasadh, Second Harvest or Mabon then Samhain and back once more to the Winter Solstice or Yule ceremony and festivities.

A sound bought Demi back to the present, Fin came into the kitchen, walking up to Demi and Oak he put his arms around them both and gave each of them in turn a good morning kiss.

"It looks as though it will be another freezing cold day today. I had better get out and about and check on the old folks on the hill, their pipes may be frozen again." Fin and Demi as custodians of the village helped everyone who needed it and as the winter freeze continued the elderly were particularly vulnerable.

"Yes, you must do that, there is some porridge on the hob, eat up before you go out and about."
After breakfast Fin left to check on the vulnerable elderly villagers and Demi began to tidy the cottage. Later she would go outdoors to gather some holly, ivy and mistletoe from the hillside and orchard and hedgerows to decorate the cottage and to make a Yule wreath in preparation for the Mid-Winter Solstice festival in a few days' time. As in many of the village households Demi had spent the past few weeks making cakes, puddings, and chutneys ready to share at the feast that followed the Winter Solstice ceremony and the Oak and Holly Kings battle in the orchard.

Later that morning Demi called to Oak, "Oak. Get your coat and gloves on it is time we went out to collect some greenery to decorate the cottage for the Winter Solstice." Oak came running already dressed for the outdoors, Demi wondered again at the child's ability to know what she was thinking and about to say. Demi collected her secateurs and a large willow basket as they made their way out of the cottage.

Demi and Oak made their way up to the top of the village to the very edge of the woodlands. There grew the old Hags, the old holly plantation that had been planted many, many years ago to supplement the winter cattle feed and for the deer to browse on. * Each year the villagers came to help themselves to the spiky plant to decorate homes and the village hall. This also helped to pollard the trees and to ensure that the trees thrived. No trees were ever cut down as it was thought that this would bring bad fortune to the village and especially those who would chop down the trees.

Demi reflected on the custom of planting a Holly tree outside a home. It was thought that Holly would protect the property from lightning and malevolent forces from entering the home and so ensure that fairies and humans could coexist under the same roof without friction during the cold months of the year. Before cutting any greenery from any tree or hedgerow Demi and Oak spent a short time in silence beside the tree and then they gave thanks to the Goddess and the spirits of the trees and hedges for giving so willingly of their branches and berries.

"Careful now mind your fingers, those spines and spikes are very sharp," Demi cautioned Oak as his eager little hands helped to place the Holly boughs into the basket.

"There are lots of berries this year. We mustn't take too much, or the birds will go hungry," observed Oak.

"Yes. I think that will be plenty. The weather is so harsh we need to leave food for the birds," Demi agreed.

"We can't eat the berries can we Mummy, only the birds may eat them."

"Yes, that is right, the berries can make humans very poorly indeed, unless you know the best way to prepare them, so it's best we leave them for the wildlife. The blackbirds and redwings especially love them," said Demi.

"Now come on, let's go back to the orchard so we can collect some mistletoe and ivy before we go home to get warm." Demi led the way back down the hill to ensure that Oak didn't slip and fall in the treacherous conditions.

Once in the orchard Demi and Oak joined several other families who were also busily harvesting mistletoe from their

3

own family apple tree. Each family had their own apple tree, they took care of the tree and carried out essential pruning and checked the tree for any signs of disease and they harvested the mistletoe that grew from the branches. When the mistletoe was cut great care was taken so the branches did not touch the ground as mistletoe is a magical parasitic plant of the air. Demi would hang some of the mistletoe over the front door as once again mistletoe is thought to protect the home from thunder and lightning and malevolent spirits.

Lastly Demi went to the hedgerow that enclosed the orchard and gathered some ivy so that Oak and Demi could make garlands and swags of holly, ivy, and mistletoe to decorate the fireplace and walls in the cottage, Demi had already made the base of her Yule wreath** and they would decorate it with more greenery.

Just as Oak and Demi reached the cottage Fin arrived. "Goodness, you have both had a very busy morning," said Fin as he surveyed the basket full of greenery that Demi had placed just inside the cottage door.

"Yes, we shall have a busy afternoon too, making swags and garlands," Fin picked up a piece of mistletoe and running up to Demi puckered up his lips for a kiss, "'Ere, give us a kiss lady!" Demi playfully kissed Fin, then, "If you have finished with that, please could you hang it over the threshold of the front door."

"Ah yes. We must protect our home from storms over the Solstice time," replied Fin. Fin found a small piece of string and tied the mistletoe to the hook above the threshold outside of the front door.

"When will you be digging up our fir tree for us to decorate ready for the festivities?" Demi asked Fin. "Probably tomorrow and we can put it up outside for a day or so and bring it in for the festivities before replanting it again."

"When we have finished hanging the greenery, we need to make some peanut garlands to hang on the tree so that the birds may enjoy them when the tree is replanted," said Demi.

"Ooo, can I help?" cried Oak in excitement.

"Yes of course you may," laughed Demi. "Now it's lunchtime. Soup is ready. Wash your hands…. both of you!"

After lunch, Fin left to help carry out some repairs to one of the cottages after a pipe had burst in the extreme weather. Demi and Oak began to make the Yule wreath and the swags of greenery for the walls of the cottage. Once the greenery had been hung the cottage was filled with the scent of pine, and the red berries on the holly shone out from the green leaves. The whole cottage took on a magical, festive, cosy feel.

"Can we make the peanut garlands now please Mummy?"

"The nuts are in the porch and the string is in the kitchen drawer we shall need a sharp skewer too and scissors. You fetch the nuts, and I will get the rest of the things we need," replied Demi.

Oak and Demi spent the rest of the afternoon making the peanut garlands. Demi made the holes in the soft shell of the peanuts and Oak carefully threaded the string through the holes. By the time they had finished they had several strings of peanuts ready to decorate their tree for the birds to feast on at the hungry time of the year. Oak could hardly wait for Fin to come home so that he could show him the decorations that he and Demi had made and the peanut garlands.

The next morning was once again very cold and frosty. Oak was up very early and rushed into Demi and Fin's room, "Daddy! When are we going to dig up the tree for Winter Solstice?" Fin and Demi opened their eyes as Oak's excited voice filled their room.

"Oh, as soon as we can after breakfast," laughed Fin. "I just hope that the ground isn't too frozen for me to dig. If it is we shall have to decorate the small fir tree in our back garden instead." Oak's face fell. "Oh, but Daddy we really need a tree indoors as we won't have anywhere to put our Yule gifts." Oak was very proud and feeling very grown up, as this year, for the first time ever, he had carefully decorated a wooden coaster for Fin's mead cup as a small gift. "Well, we shall have to see what happens when we go outside to select our tree. Come on now as we are wide awake it's time we all had a cuppa and some breakfast. Off you go and get dressed young man," said Fin. Oak rushed off to his room and soon appeared downstairs fully dressed and sat up to the table ready for breakfast.

After breakfast Fin, Demi and Oak set off for the small fir tree plantation on the hillside, after some time selecting a suitable small tree Fin began to dig. The ground was very hard and still frozen. "It's no good, I don't think I shall be able to dig a tree for this year," said Fin looking at Oak. "I'm sorry lad but the ground is just not going to thaw out in time this year." Oak looked at Demi and Fin, tears beginning to form, and his lip began to quiver, then suddenly he began to smile. "I know, can we collect some nice fallen twigs and cut a few of the pine tree branches and then take them home to put in Mummy's large pottery vase and we can decorate that instead. We can wrap some brown paper around the vase, and I can draw some lines to look like a tree trunk. We can hang our small decorations on the branches."

Demi and Fin looked at one another, they were so proud of their son, his really grown-up sensible solution to the problem took them by surprise, but of course one day Oak would take over the role of Lord of the Wildwood when Fin and Demi decided that the time was right for them to leave the village.

"Well done son, what a great idea," said Fin. They spent some time on the hill carefully selecting some attractive fallen branches. When they had looked several large branches from the pine trees littered the hillside, the recent storms and the snows had bought down some of the weakened branches. They set off home with their haul. As soon as they reached the cottage Oak rushed indoors and went to the cupboard where Demi kept the pottery vase she used for large flower displays during the summer months, "See this is the one," said Oak pointing. Demi lifted the heavy vase from the cupboard.

"You know, I think this will be perfect. Just what we need. This will look amazing when it is all set up and decorated. I have had a really good idea for the tree trunk too. How about we go back outdoors, and you do a bark rubbing using some of those wax crayons you have upstairs. I have some light brown paper. If you use a dark brown crayon, I am sure it will look really good." Oak dashed upstairs and in no time at all reappeared with his crayon set. He selected a dark brown crayon and headed for the door, "Come on Mummy!"

"On my way," replied Demi laughing at her son's enthusiasm.

Demi and Oak headed for the orchard, Oak soon found the perfect tree with a nice, patterned trunk, "Now Mummy, if you hold the paper in place I can do the bark rubbing," Demi smiled to herself. Yes, her son was certainly a force of nature and one day would be able to fill his father's role as Lord of the Wildwood. His love of the natural world and his common-sense approach and practical ability was exactly what was needed. Soon Oak had finished the bark rubbing to his satisfaction and Demi and Oak headed for home. As soon as they arrived home Fin set about making some hot chocolate for all of them.

"Just what we need after a morning out in the cold," said Fin. "Mmm, yummee," replied Oak as he wiped a chocolatey moustache from his top lip with the back of his hand and then of course wiped his hand on his trousers. Demi smiled, is it any wonder he is always filthy, she said to herself. Still, she would much rather have him out and about getting dirty and discovering more of the natural world every day than sitting at home keeping clean.

Fin downed the last of his hot chocolate, "Right who is ready to help arrange and decorate our home-made Yule tree?"

"Me! Me!" said Oak leaping to his feet.

"I think we should secure the bark rubbing to the vase first, so we don't disturb the twigs when they are in place," said Demi. "Good thinking Mummy," agreed Fin. Soon with the aid of some dark brown twine the paper bark rubbing was held firmly in place.

"Now for the fun part, come on Oak you begin arranging the twigs and green boughs," encouraged Fin. After much arranging and rearranging to get things looking just right Oak stood back and proclaimed the 'Tree' was perfect.

"Now it is time to add our small wooden decorations. I have also found some dried pine cones left over from making the Yule wreath so we can carefully tie those on too," said Demi.

After the tree was decorated Oak, Demi and Fin stood back to admire their handiwork. "Well for an alternative tree that looks pretty amazing," said Fin.

"I think that everyone in the village will want one now," said Oak.

"Well, you could be right about that," agreed Fin. "The ground is so frozen no one will be able to dig a tree this year that's for sure."

"Mummy, shall we hang the peanut garlands on our little fir tree in the garden?" asked Oak.

"Yes, we can but I have another idea too that would be lovely for the birds," replied Demi. "We still have some left-over fir cones and as they have been indoors in the warm they are all fully open. We can make a lard and seed mix to put inside them and then hang those out for the birds too."

"Oh yes! Can we do it now…. please?" Demi laughed; Oak was so enthusiastic about everything he did.

"Yes, come on, it's quite messy so we will do it in the kitchen." Demi and Oak headed towards the kitchen whilst Fin tidied up the pine needles that had fallen on the floor during the tree making and decorating.

"Now while I melt the lard you can cut some pieces of thin string so we can tie it to the fir cones," instructed Demi. Oak picked up the string, "This long?" asked Oak holding up the string. "A bit longer than that, the string needs to be long enough to go around the cone, tie to the cone and then make a loop to hang it from the tree. You need about this much,"

Demi picked up the string and cut off a length of string about ten inches or so long. Soon Oak had all the cones prepared with string.

"Here is the seed and lard mix all ready. Grab a spoon and we will start filling the cones." Soon the kitchen was filled with laughter as Oak and Demi filled up the cones.

"Now, when they are full, we need to place them upside down while the mix sets. Here let's put them in this empty egg carton they will fit inside the egg-shaped spaces just right." In no time at all there were a dozen cones drying in the egg carton, "We need to pop these in the fridge for an hour or so before we take them outside to hang up for the birds," said Demi. Oak carefully carried the egg box to the fridge and Demi helped him to place the box on the shelf.

"Mummy," whispered Oak, "When can I put Daddy's present under the tree?"

"How about later, after lunch when he has gone out to help finish off the repair to Anna's roof.

After Fin had gone out Oak excitedly fetched Fin's present from its hiding place in his bedroom and then carefully hid it behind the trunk of the tree, smiling at Demi as he did so and putting his finger to his lips making a "Shh" sound.

"Don't worry your secret is safe with me. I won't show it to Daddy. Now it is time to decorate the garden tree with the peanut garlands and seed cones."

Oak and Demi went out into the garden, the fir tree was covered in snow. After brushing away the snow Demi and Oak hung the peanut garlands and some of the seeded cones onto the tree. Just as they had finished a small movement caught Demi's eye.

"Look Oak," Demi whispered, "A robin is already eyeing up our handiwork."

Sure enough the robin sat in the hedge just waiting for them to go indoors so he could have the first pickings of the bounty laid out before him. Oak and Demi went indoors and went to the kitchen window to watch. Soon the robin was joined by blackbirds and blue tits all eager to supplement their diet with the feast that Oak and Demi had put ready for them.

"It is the Winter Solstice tomorrow…." began Demi.

"Yes, and it's my birthday too don't forget!" cried Oak excitedly.

"How could I possibly forget!" exclaimed Demi. "Now I expect that you would like a special cake to help celebrate?" Demi continued.

"Oh Yes! YES! Please."

"Well, I need to get baking so you sit quietly and play with your train set whilst I am busy in the kitchen."

"Can I help?" asked Oak.

"No, it's a surprise, Daddy will be home soon so I need to get the cake in the oven before I begin supper. Off you go."

Once again there was a hard frost overnight, Demi and Fin were up very early to prepare for the Winter Solstice ceremony before an over excited Oak came downstairs. Small gifts to exchange for the Winter Solstice had been hidden under the tree after Oak had gone to bed. There was a small separate pile of presents for Oak's birthday surprises. Demi had stayed up late to decorate Oak's cake, it was now ready for him to find on the kitchen table.

Demi and Fin had just finished gathering the Altar cloth, staffs and elemental candles as they heard Oak jump out of bed. Within a few minutes he appeared fully dressed and almost bursting with excitement.

"Mummy! Daddy! I'm up and it's my birthday and the Winter Solstice and the Holly and Oak king fight and the feast, and, and everything!" Oak cried as he erupted into the room.

Demi and Fin couldn't help laughing as their son finally ran out of breath. "Yes, yes, we know. Come and sit down, do you want to open presents first or have breakfast?"

"Presents please," much excitement followed as Oak opened his birthday gifts. "Oh, thank you Mummy and Daddy," Oak rushed over to Demi and Fin to give each of them a huge hug.

"You need to thank Grannie and Grandad when you see them later," said Demi.

"Ooo yes the ceremony, can we have breakfast now I'm starving," said Oak as he headed for the kitchen. "Cake! Thanks Mummy, it looks yummy," shouted Oak in excitement as he saw the cake sitting ready on the kitchen table. "When can we cut it?"

"Well, I think that as we have such a busy day we could cut it after breakfast and have a small piece each," said Demi.

"And we can take a piece for Granny and Grandad too…." began Oak just as there was a knock on the door.

"Winter Solstice Blessings and Happy Birthday to Oak!" Mike and Sarah walked into the kitchen.

"Grannie! Grandad!" cried Oak, "We are just going to cut my birthday cake, you can have some too."

Mike and Sarah smiled at their grandson's welcome. "Oh, and thank you so much for my lovely present," this as Oak rushed to give Sarah and Mike a hug in turn.

"Come on sit up to the table everyone. The kettle has boiled it is time for a celebration breakfast," said Demi.

After a hearty breakfast everyone left for the orchard. Already there was a large crowd gathered in the half-light waiting for the ceremony to begin. Those chosen to be the Oak and Holly Kings were ready dressed in their costumes. The trestle table used for the Altar was already set up and Fin and Mike spread the large heavy cloth over it. The elemental candles were placed ready to light and holly, ivy and mistletoe swags were placed around and onto the Altar.

Fin and Demi took their places and raised their hands for silence. "Welcome friends. Welcome to our Winter Solstice ceremony. Winter Solstice Blessings to all."

"*Winter Solstice Blessings*," replied all present.

"Today we celebrate the return once more of the Sun," at this Demi lit all the candles upon the Altar. Fin went to all the elemental points in turn.

"We welcome the Element of the East. This new day dawns. The element of pure and sacred Air is all around us. Hail and Welcome!"

"Hail and welcome!"

"We welcome the element of the South. The element of cleansing and warming fire. Hail and welcome!"

"Hail and welcome!"

"We welcome the element of the West. The element of pure, clear and cleansing Water. Clean water upon which all life on Earth depends. Hail and Welcome!"

"Hail and Welcome!"

"We welcome the element of the North. The sacred Earth, our mother, the great Bear. We walk upon you. We till your soils to grow our crops. We revere you. Hail and Welcome!"

"Hail and welcome!"

Finally, Fin and Demi raised their staffs high into the air. Together they said, "We welcome the Spirit of this sacred place. Hail and welcome!"

"Hail and welcome!"

"Now my friends turn and welcome the sunrise upon this special day. The Crone has once more given of herself and our Sun is reborn. The days will soon begin to get longer and the nights shorter, Blessed Be!"

"Blessed be!"

Everyone turned and waited eagerly for the Sun to rise. Very gradually the horizon turned from pale cream and pink to fiery oranges and reds and then the Sun burst over the horizon and flooded the orchard with weak winter sunlight. Everyone cheered. Drums began to beat and those present began to dance and sway to the drumbeat.

When the sun had risen higher in the sky Fin and Demi once again raised their hands in the air for quiet, the drums became silent, and everyone listened to Demi and Fin.

"Once again we have welcomed the return of the Sun. We

give thanks to the element of the Earth in the North. The element of Water in the West. The element of Fire in the South and the element of Air in the East. We give thanks to the Spirit of Place for allowing us to hold our sacred ceremony here today. Hail and Farewell!"

"Hail and Farewell!"

"Merry meet, merry part, merry meet again. This ceremony is now over, and our circle may be broken, Blessed Be."

"Blessed Be."

"Now let us clear away our Altar and let the battle of the Holly and Oak Kings commence," said Fin. Several helped to clear away the Altar and to make the area ready for the battle.

"Who has safe keeping of the Holly and Oak crowns?" asked Fin.

"I do," replied Demi. Demi stepped forward with the crowns which she placed upon the heads of the Holly and Oak Kings. Once the crowns were in place Demi declared.

"Let this battle of the trees of the greenwood commence. May they do honour to our woodland. May the Oak King rise as the Holly King begins to fade."

The kings battled this way and that. The sounds of the wooden staffs clashing together in the clear morning air echoed around the orchard as the crowd watched. At last, the Holly King surrendered to the might of the Oak King by kneeling at his feet.

"Who will come and take the Holly King's crown for safe keeping?" asked Fin. To the amazement of the crowd Oak stepped forward.

"I shall!" Oak walked to the kneeling Holly King and removed the crown from his head and held it aloft for all to see, "I shall keep this safe until the Summer Solstice and the next battle."

Everyone cheered and the Oak King was paraded around the orchard on the shoulders of the young men of the village. Demi and Fin went to Oak, "Well done son. Today you have carried out your first duty. You have shown the people of the village that you will one day be worthy to be custodian of our special village when your mother and I decide that it is the time for us to leave." Suddenly music rang out and the Morris dancers began to dance around the orchard. Everyone began clapping and singing. Demi and some of the other village women disappeared to ensure all was ready for the Solstice feast in the village hall. Later at a signal from Demi one of the Morris dancers beat long and loud on his drum. When everyone was quiet Fin said, "Now it is time for our Solstice feast. Let our young crown bearer and our Oak King lead us all to the village hall." Everyone followed Oak and the Oak King to the hall. When everyone was seated, and drinks had been poured Fin raised his glass to call the toast. "Winter Solstice greetings. Wassail!"

"Winter Solstice Greetings. Wassail."

Echoed everyone, Fin remained on his feet, "Now to feast. To honour our long tradition, first to be served will be our ladies who have worked long and hard to provide us with this repast. Servers make ready."

After everyone had eaten their fill the Morris dancers struck up their music once again and the singing and dancing went on long into the night. Oak couldn't remember Fin carrying him home and putting him in his bed, sweet dreams filled his sleep at the end of a magical day.

* I had no idea until I was researching this, that holly was, and in some places still is, grown to supplement feed for cattle and sheep. It is finely chopped and added to feed as it is rich in nutrients.

**To make the base for your own Yule wreath collect some newly fallen or pollarded willow branches around three foot or one metre long. Make a ring of the branch to your chosen size. Now wrap the remaining willow branch around the willow ring in an in out type pattern. If the wreath base isn't wide enough add more willow. Secure with string.

I usually begin collecting my willow after the first storms of Autumn. I find once made, the bases will last for several years if you remove the greenery and ribbons at the end of the season and store the bases in a cool dry place. I use them throughout the year to make wreaths for various ceremonies. I also collect Pine and Alder cones when I see them and can usually pick up some greenery for free when out on a woodland walk. When you have added your cones, you can paint the tips in seasonal colours if you prefer, but I leave mine plain. Add some bright ribbons and the job is done.

CHALICE WELL
HEAD POEM

I sit at the well head, silence surrounds,
No wait. What do I hear?
Mr Robin as he gently hops from branch to branch in the old
Yew tree,
Now he is foraging for worms in the leaf litter below.

Now he sits upon the wall nearby,
Head cocked to one side,
"Do you have any crumbs for me?"
He seems to ask.

We sit in companionable silence,
Mr Robin and me,
Around the well head, dressed for the season,
I peer into the dark waters,

The waters of the well gently trickle and flow,
The well sides are covered in ferns,
Gentle green fronds,
Carefully I place my own offering to the Goddess of the well.

The old Yew towers above, its bark cracked and gnarled,
I reach out to touch this venerable giant,
The bark feels warm and comforting,
The dark green needles and bright red berries adorn the
branches.

I hear voices in the distance,
Others are approaching the well head,
I see a slight movement, Mr Robin has gone,
I too stand and walk slowly away.

A WINTER
MEDITATION - YULE

S it quietly where you won't be disturbed, take a drink to ground yourself when you return. Light a candle or some incense if appropriate, adjust your clothes and get comfortable…...
Close your eyes and begin to relax…...

When you are ready to begin concentrate on your breathing, take in a deep breath. Breathe in through your nose, take the breath deep into your body, breathe out through your mouth. Breathe in through your nose and out through your mouth, once more in through the nose and out through the mouth. Now still concentrating on your breathing begin to breathe naturally…...

Imagine getting up from your chair and putting on your coat and boots…... Now leave the house. Outside it is a winter wonderland, snow has fallen heavily overnight, and the virgin white snow stretches in front of you. Follow the outline of the path until you come to a gate…... Open the gate and walk into the field closing the gate behind you…... Now turn to your left and walk up the gentle slope towards the stream that runs through the field…... All around is silence, no birds are singing and the gentle sound of the stream as it flows over the stones and pebbles is missing…... As you reach the stream you see why it is so quiet. The surface of the stream is frozen, and the series of small waterfalls are a mass of icicles. Stand still admiring the beauty of nature…. The sun suddenly comes out from behind a cloud. The sun is dazzling on the frozen ground and the surface of the stream. The icicles glimmer and glitter like fairy lights. You stand transfixed barely breathing as you take in this wonderful sight…...As you are standing with your back towards the sun you begin to feel some warmth through your coat.......Suddenly, the surface of the stream bursts into life and the sounds of the water rushing over the stones and pebbles disturbs the silence.......Water begins to drip from the icicles on the waterfalls and you now hear bird song. A blackbird comes down to drink. Soon the whole of the field is filled with birds, look up at the clear blue sky, starlings swoop and swirl in an aerial dance. Sunlight reflecting off their open wings makes them seem to shimmer like copper in the bright mid-winter sun.......Now as you look towards the top of the field you see rabbits have scraped away the snow from the surface of the grass and are intently nibbling. Suddenly they begin to rush and caper around the top of the field as though playing a game of tag. They rush and hop chasing one another in a flurry of paws and snow.......As you watch the rabbits playing you see a fox creeping towards the chasing rabbits.......The rabbits stop and in an instant, they have disappeared into their burrows, it seems the fox will be going hungry for a while longer. As you watch the fox turns and disappears back the way it had come. You realise that you are feeling hungry and thirsty. It is time you made your way back home, back the way you came. Walk back across the field towards the gate.......Open the gate, walk through the gate, and close the gate behind you.......Now walk back along the path towards home.......Go inside and take off your boots and coat. Now go back to your chair and sit.......

When you are ready to return slowly begin count down from five, move your shoulders and head from side to side as you come back to the room. If you lit a candle when you blow it out send love and healing to those in need, take a moment to reflect upon the season. Take some small sips of water to ground yourself.

FESTIVE NUT ROAST - SERVES FOUR

200g pack of chestnut puree
1 onion, finely chopped
2 cloves of garlic, smashed and chopped
2 slices of brown bread from a large loaf, blitz into breadcrumbs
A handful each of fresh sage and rosemary, blitz. Or 1 dessert spoon dried herbs
100g cranberries, fresh or frozen, leave whole
120g nuts of choice, blitz
1 heaped teaspoon yeast extract
1 heaped dessert spoon yeast flakes
Oil for frying
Ground black pepper

Fry the onion and garlic until opaque not brown.
While the onion and garlic are cooking place the rest of the ingredients into a bowl
Add the yeast extract to the onion and enough water to make the extract dissolve, not too much, around 2 tablespoons
Add the onion mix to the rest of the ingredients and mix well. As the yeast extract is quite salty, I never use any salt.
Place the mix onto a lined baking sheet and form into a log shape.

Cook at 180oC for approximately 40 minutes until browned.

This can be made in advance and to save time frozen. If using frozen cranberries do not add them until the day you plan to cook the mix, add them when the mix has defrosted.

MICROWAVE YULE (CHRISTMAS PUDDING) - SERVES FOUR

I devised this recipe as I am so concerned about the amount of waste generated buying commercially made puddings. I am also very aware that to make and cook a traditional pudding takes forever, stirring and steaming and then steaming on the feast day to reheat the pudding. This also has a massive environmental impact, not to mention on our fuel bills!

70g frozen or fresh cranberries, or ready-made sauce
1 heaped dessert spoon granulated sugar
1 heaped dessert spoon golden syrup
2 teaspoons water

150g mixed dried fruits. I use 30g mixed peel, 30g chopped glace cherries and make up the remainder with what I have to hand.
2 dessert spoons brandy, or orange juice if you prefer.

50g soft brown sugar
50g vegan margarine
50g self-raising flour
1 level dessert spoon mixed spice
1 heaped dessert spoon black treacle
1 heaped dessert spoon cocoa powder
1 eating apple peeled and grated
¼ teaspoon baking powder

Grease a 1.5-pint pudding basin

Put all the dried fruit into a small bowl and add the brandy. Stir well and set aside. If you can do this a couple of hours, or the day, before you make the pudding so much the better.

Place the cranberries with 2 teaspoons of water in a bowl and microwave on high (900w) for 2 1/2 minutes if cooking from frozen. If fresh this time will be a little less. When the berries have popped and look "jammy" add the sugar and golden syrup. Stir well and set aside to cool slightly.

Put all the other ingredients into a mixing bowl and mix until all combined.

Put 2/3 of the cranberry jam into the bottom of your greased pudding basin. Add the rest of the jam to the pudding mixture. Stir well. The mix should be a nice consistency, if too dry add a little vegan milk. Do not make the mix too sloppy.

Pour the mix into your pudding basin and cover with baking parchment. Cook on medium power (600w) for 5 1/2 minutes

Stand the pudding for 2 minutes. When you check the pudding, it should just about leave the side of the basin. If the pudding looks a little under cooked, cook for one more minute

Turn out the pudding and enjoy with vegan custard, ice cream or cream. Or all three!!

My microwave has a full power capacity of 900w and medium power 600w. If yours is different you will need to vary cooking times. I also use a plastic basin to cook my cranberries and pudding. If you use glass basins the cooking time will increase slightly.

FESTIVE YULE TREATS

There is nothing nicer than a sweet treat to help to clear the gloom of a long winter afternoon or evening.
These could also be popped into pretty boxes or decorated jars to give as gifts.

DATE SURPRISES

1 glove box of dates
Plain marzipan

Remove the stones from the dates by cutting them lengthwise. Carefully roll some of the marzipan into a thin sausage shape. Cut a piece just a little shorter than the cut in the date and place the marzipan roll inside the date.

MARZIPAN CHOCOLATES

Bar of plain vegan chocolate.
Marzipan
Wooden skewer
Baking parchment

Cut the marzipan into small pieces and slowly melt the chocolate in a bowl over a pan of simmering water, ensure the bowl does not touch the water. While the chocolate is melting, roll each piece of marzipan into a ball about ½ inch in diameter. When the chocolate has melted pierce the marzipan with the skewer and dip into the melted chocolate. Place onto the baking parchment to set.

If you prefer you can cut the marzipan into ½ squares instead.

CHOCOLATE BRAZIL NUTS

Dip whole Brazil nuts into melted chocolate. Set aside to set.

CHOCOLATE FESTIVE SHAPES

Many cook shops sell a selection of silicone festive shaped ice cube makers. I have found they make great moulds to make chocolates and they don't need to be greased.

Melt some vegan chocolate of your choice, plain, milk or white or all three in different bowls, over a pan of simmering water. 1 level dessert spoon into your mould makes a very generous sized chocolate. Whilst the chocolate is still soft sprinkle with dried cranberries or chopped crystalised ginger, chopped almonds etc. you can put two different types of chocolate together and gently swirl with a skewer to mix slightly to make a ripple effect. The choice is yours.

Enjoy.

IMBOLC

A VILLAGE TALE

*W*e welcome our restored Maiden Goddess at Imbolc. New life springs forth, the first stirrings of Spring abound. Snowdrops carpet the ground and pussy willow and hazel catkins decorate bare branches. New lambs in the fields romp and play until the ewes call them to their side.

Demi yawned and stretched. Her neck and shoulders ached, as she got out of bed her hips were painful and her knees cracked. At last, it was the day of her rebirth as the Maiden Goddess at Imbolc. After yet another very cold and harsh winter, with snow lying on the ground for several weeks, a thaw had finally set in last evening and already the temperature felt much warmer. Demi struggled downstairs just as the dawn was beginning to break. Demi reached for her thick cloak and after pulling it on around her shoulders she pulled up the hood and left the cottage. Demi shuffled through the village street and then up through the orchard for the final stage of her journey. She had to climb up the boulder strewn path to the Glade. Finally, she made it. Kneeling at the edge of the stream that was in full flow now the thaw had set in, she bathed her face and hands in the icy cold waters. As she bathed her hands, she could see the arthritic changes disappearing and as she saw her reflection in the water, she could see that her face was once more youthful and unlined and her hair had transformed from silvery white to her usual fiery red.

After bathing Demi sat for a while on one of the many boulders. As she sat the birds began to sing. The sweet songs of the robin and blackbird filled the Glade. As Demi watched the blackbirds began to feed on some of the remaining holly berries, when they saw Demi, they began to scold as only blackbirds seem able to.

When she was feeling rested and stronger Demi stood to leave the Glade just as Oak erupted into the clearing followed by Fin.

"Mummy, you are all young again," cried Oak.

"Yes, I am once more restored which is as well so that I can keep up with you young man," laughed Demi.

For the first few years after he was born Oak had not really noticed that Demi's appearance changed throughout the year but of recent times, he had been curious why Demi had seemed to really age after the Winter Solstice. Now that he was six, he wanted to know what was happening to his mother each year.

"Mummy, why do you get so old and grey and then so young again every year?"

Fin and Demi had already decided that it was time that Oak understood what was happening to Demi so with a nod from Fin Demi began.

"Many years ago, I agreed to become daddy's wife and Consort and to become The Lady of the Greenwood, The Lady of the Land and Harvest, to daddy's Lord of the Greenwood, Lord of the Wildhunt. You are old enough now to realise that in this village we follow the Path of the Wheel of the Year and honour nature and welcome the new Sun God at the Winter Solstice or Yule. You also know that for daddy and I to be able to fulfil our roles we cannot leave the boundaries of the village after sunset or before sunrise or we shall begin to age and will not be able to act as Guardians and Custodians of the village. As a part of this in my role of Lady of the Land and Harvest I raise your father each year after he has been slain by the corn scythes. Daddy's blood has to be spilt upon our Mother, the Earth to ensure that the crops will flourish again the following year. In my turn, as Lady of the Land and Harvest, in the late autumn my powers begin to fade and the land sleeps and rests. The trees lose their leaves, and the fields are barren of crops as they too rest. From the Winter Solstice onwards, after we have welcomed the rebirth of our God the Sun, I too fade and age to become the Crone. I am reborn as the new Maiden Goddess when the birds begin to sing once more. When the trees begin to show the beginnings of the buds for new leaves and the snowdrops begin to push their way up through the earth and show green shoots. Then I bathe in the snow swollen waters of the Glade and my youth and beauty is restored once more. As the Sun God gains his strength and becomes higher in the sky and his warmth stronger, I become the Mother of the woodland and of the crops in the fields and the Mother of the harvest when the Wheel has turned once again for this is the way of things. This is the way nature works and man interferes with it at his peril."

Whilst Demi was speaking Oak had been uncharacteristically quiet, his head to one side, he had listened intently to everything Demi had said.

"But Mummy does this mean that you will never, ever die?"

Fin took over, "No lad we shall both die one day. One day we shall leave the village and we shall live in the cottage over the hill that we visit sometimes. When we leave the village, we shall age at a normal rate and in the distant future we shall both die together on the same day at the same time."   Once again Oak had been silent.

"So, Daddy does that mean that will be when I take over responsibility for the village?" asked Oak.

"Yes, lad it does but that won't be for many years yet. Before then you need to learn how to be responsible. How to recognise and look after the trees, hedgerows, and wildlife. How to repair and to mend. How to raise and harvest crops and how to lead the ceremonies and festivals as the years unfold," at this Oak looked very serious.

"But Daddy will I ever be ready for such a huge job?"

"Yes of course, as Mummy and I will be helping you and guiding you every step of the way." Oak nodded, "Is it time for breakfast now?" Demi and Fin laughed, "Yes come on it's pancakes this morning. I made the batter earlier," said Fin.

With their son between them Demi and Fin left the Glade. As Demi walked back through the woodland and the orchard the remaining snow melted and the snowdrops that had bravely pushed leaves through the frozen ground began to flower. Some early bumblebees hovered over the snowdrops as the sun appeared from behind a cloud, the sky turned the wonderful clear blue it only does in late winter. The bare branches of the apple trees were still covered in the remains of mistletoe, the berries were long gone, and the leaves had turned a yellowy green as it began to fade. Everywhere there was the air of expectation. Of the feeling that new life and growth was soon coming.

"So, Mummy does this mean that the winter is now over and gone?" asked Oak.

"Oh no far from it. This is just the first stirrings, the very beginning of new life. We shall still have hard frosts and possibly some more snow for a few weeks yet. But Spring is on the way."

After breakfast Fin and Oak decided to make the most of the glorious morning. By now the sun was shining from a clear blue sky and it felt warm, almost Springlike.

"Daddy, can we go for a walk up to the fields above the village?" asked Oak.

"Yes, why not. Let's make the most of the lovely day. Are you coming too?" Fin asked Demi.

"I need to meditate and to prepare for the ceremony later today. You boys go off and enjoy your walk." Leaving Demi at the cottage Fin and Oak made for the fields.

It was indeed a wonderful day. As Fin and Oak approached the fields, they could see several new lambs gambolling and playing tag, their newborn lamb coats brilliant white against the blue sky. Oak and Fin stopped at the gate admiring the lambs and laughing at their antics.

Suddenly Oak asked, "Is that sheep OK daddy?"

Fin looked to where Oak was pointing, "No son she looks to be in trouble. Well spotted. Come on climb over the gate let's see what the problem is." Fin was already suspecting that the sheep was having trouble delivering her lamb. Fin and Oak knelt by the sheep.

"Steady girl," said Fin calmly. He could see that the toes of one hoof were sticking out of the birth canal, but the sheep was straining too hard and that something was amiss. "We shall have to help the old girl to deliver this lamb as by the time we have called the farmer or a vet the lamb will be dead." Fin very gently felt inside the sheep. Immediately he found the problem. One of the lambs feet was the correct way round, but the other leg was bent right back. Fin very carefully slid his hand along to the lamb's shoulder to find the foot and then very gently, keeping his hand between the hoof and the birth canal, so that he didn't damage the sheep, carefully moved the leg forward into the correct position. "Right lass one more push and your lamb should be born," suddenly with a gush of fluid the lamb was born. "Phew that's a relief. I thought for a minute the lamb may be dead. It was also a good thing that there was a fair amount of fluid in the birth canal, and it wasn't dry or I would have damaged the sheep."

"Daddy you are so clever. Look at the ewe she is busily cleaning her lamb," said Oak excitedly.   "Yes, that helps to stimulate the lamb to breathe. Soon it will be getting onto his wobbly legs and begin to feed." Sure, enough within a few minutes the lamb was feeding and seemed to have no ill effects from its traumatic journey into the world.

"Look Daddy is the sheep having another lamb?" Fin checked the ewe again, "Yes. It looks as though she is having twins. Let's just wait a little while and check that this one is born without needing any help." Fin and Oak waited near the ewe, within a few minutes the next lamb was born easily, and the ewe began to clean up the second lamb, very soon it too was on its feet feeding. Oak watched the whole thing with a smile on his face.

"Nature is a wonderful thing daddy," said Oak.

"It surely is, the placenta, the thing that nourishes the lamb when it is inside it's mother's womb, will be born later. I have heard that sometimes the ewe will eat the placenta, but I have never seen a sheep do it. Foxes and other scavengers will come and clear it up to feed to their babies."   Fin and Oak gave a final check to the sheep and her lambs before heading home. The lambs, now full from their first feeds were resting, and the ewe was beginning to graze.

Oak and Fin made their way across the fields and back down towards the village and home. As they passed the orchard, they could see that there was a lot of activity as everyone was beginning to gather to make preparations for the ceremony to welcome the first stirrings of Spring. By the time they had reached their cottage Demi was ready for the ceremony and dressed in a gown of white with a sash of pale green. On her head was a circlet of ivy leaves.

"You have cut it fine, I thought that you weren't going to make it back in time, is everything OK?" asked Demi.

"Mummy, Mummy, we helped to deliver a baby lamb up in the top field!" cried Oak excitedly, "And we couldn't leave until we knew the sheep and her lambs were OK."

"Goodness me what happened?" asked Demi. "Tell me whilst I help you change for the ceremony."

Oak and Demi disappeared upstairs to Oak's room Fin could hear Oak explaining to his mother what had happened while he in turn made himself ready for the ceremony.

In a few minutes they were ready to make their way to the orchard. When they reached the gate to the orchard, they could see that the Altar had been set and covered with a white cloth and decorated with ivy and white and pale green ribbons, pots of snowdrops and the symbols of the elements of Earth, Air, Fire and Water. Fin and Oak left Demi at the orchard gate and went to join the rest of the crowd waiting for the ceremony to begin. In a few minutes the ceremony got underway. Demi's attendants escorted her to the Altar and presented her with her staff which was also decorated in white and pale green ribbons. Demi raised her staff in the air for silence.

"Today we celebrate the first stirrings of Spring. The first flowering of the snowdrops. The snow has now melted on the high moors above and the wind has changed direction." Everyone looked towards the high moors and yes, indeed the snow had melted, and it did feel milder. The brilliant blue sky from earlier had now faded and the sky was rapidly turning grey with a threat of rain.   "Now that I am restored to you once more as the Lady of the Land and Harvest, I ask the Guardians of the Air, of the East to bless our village as this new growing year begins. I ask the Guardians of Fire of our sacred Sun God of the South to bless our village as this new growing year begins. I ask the Guardians of the Water, of the West to bless our village as this new growing year begins, may pure clear waters nurture us and all life and bring forth sweet gentle rains to water our crops. I ask the Guardians of the North, of our sacred Earth, our Great Mother to bless the crops that we sow and bring forth a bumper harvest in the Summer and Autumn. I welcome the Spirit of this orchard, the Spirit of our Sacred Space Blessed Be."

"Blessed Be." Echoed all present.

Demi continued. "As we look towards the skies the rain is beginning to fall. It is a sign, according to legend, that the Winter will soon be over if it rains upon this day. The Cailleach, the Winter Crone, will stay at home, she will not be able to go out in the rain to gather more firewood for the Winter. If she stays at home Winter will very soon be over, but before we get too excited, I am sure that the Cailleach managed to gather plenty of firewood in the beautiful warm sunshine that we had this morning."

Everyone smiled at the prospect of the end of winter, by now everyone was yearning for spring proper to begin and so herald the long warm days of summer.

Once again Demi raised her staff into the air, "This is the time of the year when we honour and bless those who heal us. Doctors, nurses, midwives. We bless those who work with fire, blacksmiths, and farriers. We thank you all for the work that you do within our village and in the wider community. May you be blessed in all that you do. Blessed Be."

"Blessed Be."

Demi continued, "It is also the time of year to sow the seeds of your own ambition. What do you wish to achieve? What are your own personal goals? Tomorrow, after the festivities of today, sit quietly and meditate, ask for guidance for the future." To everyone's amazement Oak walked to where Demi stood.

"Mummy can I say something please?" asked Oak. Demi nodded her encouragement.

"This morning mummy and daddy explained to me that one day I have to do what they do. Look after everybody who lives in our village. I don't know if I will ever know how to do it properly. I need to understand what I need to do. I need to learn lots if I am going to be as clever as daddy and mummy. This morning daddy and I helped to deliver a baby lamb, if daddy hadn't helped the lamb, it would have died. That is so very sad, and I would have been very upset. I need to learn all of this. I need to learn how to mend and repair stuff too. In the school holidays can I watch how things are done so I can learn from all the clever people in our village, please?"

Those who were craftsmen, the carpenters, roofers, plumbers all nodded.

"Aye lad," "Yes son," said another, "You come round with me on the farms," offered Richard the vet. Suddenly most of the ladies and some of the men discovered that they had something in their eye, and several were in need of a handkerchief. Oak nodded his thanks and prepared to go back to where he had been standing with Fin and his grandparents, Sarah, and Mike. Demi placed her hands upon his shoulders.

"Thank you to everyone who has offered to help Oak in his quest to learn how to become custodian of our village, of this special place. Oak realises that one day he will need to be able to help others in their time of need and to lead the village to the best of his ability." As Oak walked back to Fin several people touched his shoulders in tokens of support. When the murmurs of support had died down Demi raised her staff into the air once more.

"Now that our ceremony is over, I give thanks to the Guardians of the East, South, West and North and to the Spirit of Place. I ask each household before they leave, to take a pot of the snowdrops that are placed upon and around the Altar. Take them home and plant them in your own gardens or a place that is special to you and your family. May they grow and give pleasure to all who look upon them for many years to come. Now it is time for fun and merriment, the Morris dancers await us on the Village Green." At this everyone began to leave the orchard to watch and join in with the Morris dancing.

Demi walked towards Oak and Fin who were standing with Sarah and Mike.

"Oak has just been telling us about helping the ewe to deliver her lamb this morning," said Mike.   "Yes, he was bursting to tell me all about it when he got home just before the ceremony which is why we were a little late. He did well, I am so proud of him."

Demi looked at Fin, "And of course you too my love," said Demi with a smile. "It was a good lesson well learnt. Oak has much to learn before he will be able to take over the custody of the village," replied Fin.

"He will be more than ready when the time comes with you and Demi as his guides, and now the pledges from the craftspeople who have also offered to help and guide him on his way to adulthood," said Sarah smiling down upon her grandson.

IMBOLC

Lowering cloud, a chilly drizzly late winter day,
I follow the cobbled path to the well head to pray,
I am alone in this magical sacred garden so beloved by so many,
Quietly I sit as Robin sweetly sings.

Winter box, daphne and lonicera all planted near,
Fill the air with sweet cloying heady perfumes,
Lady and hart's tongue ferns, a splash of welcome green on
this grey day,
Winter hellebores white flowers against green leaves.

The oak tree towers above, his fallen leaves mulch the borders,
The beech hedge resplendent in his winter copper finery,
At my feet the cobbles are interspersed with ammonites,
The well head is decorated for the season.

Early snowdrops brave the day,
The new green shoots of daffodils break the earth,
Soon the borders will be covered in new spring growth,
New green shoots cover the tips of tree branches.

As I walk towards the lion's head waterspout,
I stop to admire the vibrant yellow mahonia and drink in its
perfume,
My reward? My first bumble bee of the season,
Hail and well met my friend.

I drink the healing waters,
I send blessings and healing to family and friends,
I stand to honour the Goddess of the spring,
I give thanks and leave this quiet space.

I walk to the vesica pool, stained red by the flowing waters of
the red spring,
Its beautiful shape mirrors the well head design,
As I stand at the edge, the Lady's pool reflects,
I give thanks for this sacred space.

This poem is set at the beautiful Chalice Well, Glastonbury

IMBOLC MEDITATION

S it quietly where you won't be disturbed, take a drink to ground yourself when you return. Light a candle or some incense if appropriate, adjust your clothes and get comfortable…...

Close your eyes and begin to relax…...

When you are ready to begin concentrate on your breathing, take in a deep breath, breathe in through your nose, take the breath deep into your body. Breathe out through your mouth, breathe in through your nose and out through your mouth, once more in through the nose and out through the mouth. Now still concentrating on your breathing begin to breathe naturally…...

You are walking along a quiet country lane…... It is the beginning of February; the hedgerows are lined with snowdrops. As you walk you can hear the birds beginning to sing once more. Robin, blackbird, sparrow, blue tit all are becoming aware that the days are getting longer and soon it will be time to find a mate and begin nest building……

As you continue your walk you can hear running water in the distance…...As you get closer to the sound of water you see the entrance to a wood, the gate is open. Go through the gate and turn left. The whole of the woodland floor is covered in snowdrops. The woodland is patterned by dappled sun as it bravely struggles to pierce the tree cover. At this time of the year the Sun is still feeble and weak, but he grows in strength with each passing day. You see a tree stump and decide to go and sit for a while. As you sit you see the rushing stream on your right, the water is flowing over boulders and smaller stones. The banks of the stream are also covered in snowdrops. Look carefully at the small delicate flowers, notice the three clean, pure white outer petals…...the inner white petals are tipped with green and the whole flower looks as though it is fixed to the stem by a green stopper. The beautiful green stems emerge from the leaf litter strewn on the woodland floor when the leaves fell from the trees during the autumn winds and gales. Sit here a while and enjoy admiring the carpet of pure white flowers…. Now stand and continue your walk along the woodland path. The stream is still on your right. As you walk you notice the trees that are lining the path and the banks of the stream. The trunks of the trees are all covered with thick dark green moss. In some places the moss has been rubbed off by deer. Suddenly you see a face in the trees. As you approach you see that a tree stump is covered with thick green moss. The sides of the tree stump are covered in ivy so that it almost looks like hair. At the top of the tree stump and in the middle some brown ferns from last summer linger. They look like some hair and a beard. Stop and say hello to the Green Man of the woodland…...Now continue to walk along the path. Cross over a small bridge and turn to your right so that the stream is now on your right…....The tree cover is denser here but still the woodland floor is carpeted with snowdrops. You hear a noise from one of the trees up ahead. As you approach the tree you see a large raven sitting in one of the branches. Again, the raven makes a loud cry. Stop near to the tree to admire the huge bird. The raven sits and watches you his head to one side, his sharp intelligent eyes assessing if you may be a threat……

The raven decides that you are not an enemy and sits calmly in the tree. As you decide to approach the tree you realise that it is an Alder. The tips of the branches are covered in tiny dark brown cones from last year and the new catkins that will flower in a few weeks. This beautiful tree often grows close to water and its small cones make lovely decorations for wreaths at Yule…...Now continue walking along the path. Admire the snowdrops and notice hazel and birch trees. Notice the fine tips of the branches, see how the new buds are ready to emerge in the Spring. They are waiting for the silent signal, when the weather warms, the new fresh green leaves will appear. Ahead you see the gate that led into the woodland. Walk towards the light at the end of the tree lined path.…....Now as you leave the woodland turn to your right back onto the road and walk back in the direction you came.…....

When you are ready to return slowly begin count down from five, move your shoulders and head from side to side as you come back to the room. If you lit a candle when you blow it out send love and healing to those in need and take a moment to reflect upon the season. Take some small sips of water to ground yourself.

The inspiration for this meditation is the beautiful Snowdrop Valley on Exmoor

CHUNKY VEGETABLE SOUP

1 large onion or leek sliced
2 cloves chopped garlic
1 large carrot, chopped
1 parsnip, chopped
1 potato, chopped
125g red lentils
1 can baked beans
Vegetable stock cube
1 heaped tablespoon tomato puree
1 heaped tablespoon yeast flakes
Vegetable oil
Spices or herbs

Put the chopped onion and garlic into a large saucepan and fry in a small amount of oil until transparent. If you are using spices add them now and fry for about a minute to bring out the flavour. Now add the rest of the chopped vegetables and lentils to the pan. Cover with enough water to just cover the vegetables and lentils. Bring to the boil and simmer for about 10 minutes. Now add the stock cube, tomato puree, yeast flakes and baked beans and herbs if you are using them.
You may need to add a small amount of water if the soup is a little thick. Simmer for about another 20 minutes.

Serve with cheese scones or crusty bread. I always make enough for 2 days; the soup is always better the following day.

If you don't have the vegetables, I have listed just use what you do have. I throw in whatever I have to hand. Butternut squash, courgette, green beans, sweet corn nibs etc.

This is a recipe I have been using for the whole of our married life, at the time of typing this is almost 49 years. I first used it when we were literally penniless, and I had to make a very little go a long way. To make it go further you can also throw in some pasta shapes or broken up spaghetti.

WHITE CHOCOLATE SHORTBREAD COOKIES

175g plain flour
160g vegan margarine
100g sugar
50g vegan white chocolate chopped into small pieces

Place all the ingredients into a bowl, except for the chocolate. Mix well. Add the chocolate and combine with the cookie mix. Place the dough onto some cling film and make into a log shape. Wrap in the cling film and chill for at least one hour in the fridge.

When the dough has chilled remove the cling film (put to recycle) and cut with a knife into 14 pieces. Place onto a lined baking sheet. Press down with a fork. Bake for 20 – 25 minutes at 170oC

LAMB'S WOOL DRINK

A traditional drink for Imbolc or for wassail

Place one litre of cider, or for a non-alcoholic version apple juice, into a large saucepan.

Add some soft brown or white sugar to taste then add your mulling spices. I use a teaspoon each of either ground or fresh ginger root, sweet cinnamon or a cinnamon stick and ground mixed spice. Put the ground spices into a muslin bag if you have one, if not after you have mulled the cider or juice you will need to strain it though a tea strainer or muslin square. If using a cinnamon stick or fresh ginger root place them directly into the liquid and remove afterwards by straining the liquid.

Heat the liquid very slowly until hot but not boiling.

Add to the mulled cider or juice a very well stewed apple, bramley works the best, it needs to be the consistency of apple sauce, beat in the apple just before serving.

Enjoy.

OSTARA

A VILLAGE TALE

*T*he Wheel has turned once more, Our Goddess Eostre will soon return. Hares will box, apple blossoms will adorn the trees, Bees will feast upon the sweet nectar. Children will hunt for chocolate eggs now that the Spring has returned. The old ones will give thanks that they have been spared and look forward to feeling the warmth of the Summer Sun once more.

After a very long, cold, and wet winter the days were noticeably growing longer, and to everyone's relief, much drier. Now, towards the end of the lambing season, the muddy puddles and sodden lanes and fields were beginning to dry out and gardens and allotments could be dug, and seeds sown.

The windows of the cottages and houses in the village were thrown open to allow in some much-needed sunlight and fresh warm breezes, having been firmly shut for many months against the harsh winter gales and seemingly non-stop rain. Rugs and carpets were taken outdoors to be beaten and cleaned and everywhere paintbrushes were very much in action.

The blossoms were beginning to open on the apple and cherry trees in the orchard and the ground was covered in a thick carpet of daffodils. Primroses adorned garden walls and borders and the banks of the stream and throughout the village and surrounding countryside. Now everyone's thoughts began to turn towards spring and the coming festival of Ostara or the Spring Equinox.

In the village hall Demi and Fin were busy with some of the other villagers sorting out the egg hunt signs, everyone had decided that this year there would be some new clues as the children, and adults, were so used to the old clues and egg hiding places the egg hunt was over in no time at all.

Oak had taken himself off towards the orchard and glade and woodlands and fields beyond. As ever he was keen to explore his surroundings and the natural world, at twelve years old he was becoming more adventurous and keener to learn the secrets of nature's ways. After the steep climb out of the village Oak reached the hedgerow bordered fields. The ewes and lambs were grazing contentedly whilst flocks of crows picked at the ground foraging for insects and beetles. Wood pigeons called from the trees at the top of the field their location given away by the occasional noisy flapping of their wings. A slight movement caught Oak's eye and as he looked towards the trees again, he saw a grey squirrel trying his luck at stealing one of the pigeon's eggs, the pigeons put up a good fight and for once managed to see the squirrel off. Oak knew that when a squirrel tries to raid a bird's nest the parents will often desert the nest and the eggs or baby birds will all be lost. Oak also knew that larger birds such as crows and magpies will raid the nests of smaller birds. It's not at all surprising that small birds hide their nests so well, he thought to himself.

As Oak was about to walk away another movement caught his eye. He stopped to take a second look. Yes, just there, near the hedge he saw a large brown hare, as he watched the hare sat up, her large black tipped ears pricked bolt upright. Soon another hare appeared. It was obvious that this was a male hare, and he was hoping that the female was coming into season so that he could mate with her. Sure enough, as Oak watched, the male hare approached the female and began to sniff her. The female hare began to move across the field towards Oak who was standing in the shade of the hedgerow. The male followed the female, the female was having none of it, she turned and at once reared on her hind legs and began to box the male away. The male could see that he was beaten and decided to give up for now, but Oak knew that he wouldn't go very far in the hope of better luck over the following few days.

Oak began to walk towards the woodlands at the top of the hill. The path was very wet and muddy still and Oak knew it was a good opportunity to check out what wildlife was around as there would be footprints left in the mud. The first thing he spotted was a badger track, easily identified by the distinct large back pad and separate four toe pads and four large claws. Next, he saw some fox prints, again easily identified, the tracks appear to be a single line of prints, a little like dainty dog prints. Then he saw the distinct two oblong and pointy toe or slot prints of deer, judging by the depth of the print and size it was red deer who had passed this way not the more common roe deer that was often seen in and around the village.

Oak's tummy began to rumble, time to head home it must be nearly lunchtime. Oak, in common with most children of his age, was always hungry.

Back in the village hall Demi and Fin and the other villagers were packing away the egg hunt signs and clues. Everyone was sworn to secrecy about the new egg hiding places.

"The hunt should last quite a while longer this year. This should give more time to prepare the feast and for Morris dancing," said Fin.

"Yes," agreed Demi, "And also to set up the pancake races, Hilda, and Freda, are you still happy to help prepare the pancake batter early in the morning?" Hilda and Freda nodded their agreement.

"We shall meet you here in the hall as soon as the Ostara ceremony is over, is around eight o'clock OK with you both?" asked Freda.

"Perfect," agreed Demi and Hilda together.

"Now it's time for lunch. Oak will be home soon and no doubt he will be ravenous as usual," said Demi.

"That's growing lads for you," chuckled Freda, "Young lads are like wood pigeons. Always hungry." On that note everyone left for home.

Oak arrived home a short time after Demi and Fin.

"Hello lad. Had a good morning?" asked Fin.

"Oh yes Dad. I saw two hares boxing and loads of animal footprints in the mud in the top woods."

"Ah that is good news, a sign that Spring is just around the corner at last. It's certainly been a long cold, wet and damp winter. I really can't remember one quite as bad for a great many years," said Fin.

"Lunch is ready," called Demi from the kitchen.

A few days later the Spring Equinox dawned grey and overcast. "Oh, I hope it perks up a bit," said Demi. "The Winter Solstice and Imbolc celebrations were so wet and miserable I was hoping it would be a little warmer and sunny today."

"Give it time," replied Fin, "It will clear later, and the wind has changed direction so it should be a warmer day today."

Sure enough, by the time everyone had gathered around the beautifully decorated Altar in the orchard for the Ostara or Spring Equinox ceremony the sky had begun to clear. The colours of the season were everywhere, not only on the Altar. Almost everyone was dressed in yellow, green and violet or blue. As Demi and Fin began the opening words the Sun climbed over the horizon bathing the orchard in a pink and gold light.

"Today we welcome our Spring Goddess, Eostre. We welcome the Spring. We welcome the light and warmth returning to the Land, to the Earth. May the seeds that we sow bring forth a bumper crop to feed and nurture us during next winter. We give thanks that we have been spared during the hard lean times behind us. Now as the daylight hours roughly equal that of the night-time, let us give thanks. As above so below."

"As above so below." echoed all who were present.

"Now let us welcome the Guardians of the elements." Demi, Fin, and for the first time, Oak welcomed each of the elements in turn and finally the Spirit of Place. Everyone listened to Oak as he carefully recited the traditional words and phrases. Yes, the lad would do a grand job when his turn came to lead the ceremonies.

"Now that our ceremony is over, it is time for fun and merriment. Our egg hunt is already set out for all to enjoy. This year we have set different clues and hidden the eggs in different locations. We hope that you enjoy yourselves," announced Demi.

"The Morris dancers are about to set up on the green and the pancake races will begin in an hour or so. Enjoy the day." Shouted Fin above the clamour of the excited voices of the children and adults. Everyone began to disperse. Demi headed for the village hall to meet her mother, Sarah who was waiting with Freda and Hilda to make the pancake batter. Fin and Oak and Demi's father Mike began to set up the makeshift outdoor kitchen where the pancakes would be cooked before the races began.

By the time the batter had been prepared the first children arrived back to the orchard to claim their chocolate eggs. Mike and Sarah and Oak began to hand out the eggs to the excited children. "Steady on," laughed Sarah, "There are plenty to go around."

As soon as the eggs had been handed out the wrappers were torn away, and the chocolate devoured. "You know where to put all the empty wrappers," said Mike as in their excitement some of the children had accidentally dropped some foil.

"Sorry," they managed to mumble though mouths full of chocolate.

After the egg hunt the children went to the activity tents. One was for storytelling, a task that Demi loved to do, and one was for egg painting which Sarah and Mike always oversaw.

"Do you have enough paint on your table?" asked Sarah as the first of the children arrived.

"Yes, thank you," replied the children.

"That is so pretty!" exclaimed Sarah as the first of the

eggs were finished. "Come let's hang them on the tree and you can claim them later. Don't forget to make a wish as you hang your egg on the tree." Soon the egg tree branches were full of beautiful brightly painted eggs.

"This is such a lovely tradition," said Mike.

"It is a symbol of fertility and renewal of life. The egg is such a sacred symbol as it has been for thousands of years. It is a symbol of 'Life in Potential' and we wish for what we would like to happen by the summer," said Sarah.

"The branches of the tree look so pretty with all the painted eggs. Of course, the branches of the tree must be some that have fallen naturally to the ground and never cut from a living tree at this time of the year," said Mike.

"Yes, at this time of the year it is best to leave the tree as it is as all pruning should have been done by now," agreed Sarah.

In the storytelling tent Demi was in her element. She had already told the story of the Hare and the Bird and Eostre the Goddess. Now the children were asking for another story. "This is a traditional west country tale about the Hare and the Goddess," began Demi.

"Oh, that is where we live, in the West Country," cried one of the children, Demi nodded and smiled as she began to tell the story.

"A very long, long time ago the animals heard that the Goddess was paying them a visit to celebrate the Spring or Vernal Equinox. All the animals wanted to give the Goddess a special present. Some of the animals found some gold. Others found silver or precious gems and jewels, but the poor Hare had nothing to give. Sad and alone the Hare returned to his bleak and lowly home. What could he give the Goddess? All the other animals had mocked poor Hare as he had nothing to give. As the Hare sat miserably alone, he suddenly saw a single solitary egg on the shelf. He picked up the egg and began to decorate it in bright colours. When the Goddess arrived all the other animals rushed to give her their precious gifts. The Goddess saw the Hare standing quietly alone, 'What do you have for me, my good Hare?' The Hare very shyly placed the decorated egg at the Goddess' feet. He felt very foolish as all the other animals were staring at him and his lowly gift. 'Sorry,' muttered Hare, 'It is a poor gift, but it is the only thing I had in my house.'

'But Hare it is beautiful, thank you for your gift. You have given me all that you have on the Earth. In honour of this, from today onwards you shall be my special animal, you shall for evermore be by my side as my companion animal.' All the other animals cheered the Hare in his humility and began to see that gold, silver and gems are not what is important in this life but giving what you can and helping others is what is important."

After the story all the children were quiet for a while, then, "Please Demi. Is this why we try to live as simple a life as possible in our village and only take from the land what we need and not over produce?"

"Well yes I suppose it is," said Demi, "We try to protect our environment and look after the natural world in and around the village."

"So, is this why Mike was cross when we dropped some litter earlier when we were eating our chocolate eggs?" asked another child.

"Yes, it certainly was. We should never drop litter or pollute the stream as it will kill or poison our precious wildlife or livestock."

"Do you have more stories?" asked one of the other children.

"Do you know why we eat hot cross buns?" asked Demi.

"'Cos they are scrummy and tasty especially when they are warm," the children chorused.

Demi laughed, "Well yes that is a good reason. But not exactly what I meant. Eating hot cross buns dates back at least two thousand years to Roman times. The round bun is supposed to represent the Wheel of the Year and the points of the cross symbolise the elements of Air, Earth, Fire and Water and the centre point in the middle the Spirit. It is also thought to represent a Celtic Cross."

"But why do we always eat eggs at this time of the year and why does my granny always bury an egg outside her front door?" asked one of the children.

"That is an excellent, or should I say, an eggcellent question. We eat eggs as they are a symbol of fertility and new life and new growth. The bright yellow of the egg yolk represents the sun. Your granny buries a raw egg outside near her front door, to ensure an abundant harvest and fertility in her garden. It is a very old custom and several of the villagers around the same age as your granny will follow the old tradition. Now I hear that the pancake races are about to begin. Off you go and join in the fun."

The children all dashed off towards the village green for the pancake races and of course as many pancakes as they could eat afterwards. There would be more Morris dancing and running races before everyone gathered in the village hall for the late afternoon feast just after Sunset.

OSTARA

Apple blossoms brave the blustery wind,
Skies change from brilliant blue to threatening grey,
We rush for shelter from the sudden downpour,
The sun chases away the clouds once more.

Hares box, rabbits'race, the vixen gives birth in a thorny thicket,
Birds are busy nest building,
In the distance the cuckoo calls, his voice a true herald of spring,
Soon the swallows will arrive.

The frog and toad spawn begins to hatch,
Tadpoles cling to the sides of ponds and deep puddles,
Crows feed upon this early spring bounty,
Some tadpoles hide, and as frogs and toads, emerge.

We sow seeds and plant potato tubers,
Bean poles are already in the ground,
The grass begins to grow, sounds of mowers fill the air,
Backs ache after winter's sloth.

Primroses abound, sweet perfume fills the air,
Bluebells lift their arched necks to bloom in glory,
Ferns emerge, fronds unfold from soft brown to green,
Leaves upon bare boughs begin to unfurl.

Children play, seeking chocolate eggs so cunningly hidden,
Squeals of delight fill the warming spring days,
Chocolatey faces, beaming smiles,
"Oh please, can I eat just one more?"

The coming of our Spring Goddess Eostre,
We have been waiting all winter long for Her to return,
Today we rejoice at Her re-emerging,
She is all around us as we celebrate.

OSTARA MEDITATION

S it quietly where you won't be disturbed, take a drink to ground yourself when you return. Light a candle or some incense if appropriate, adjust your clothes and get comfortable…...
Close your eyes and begin to relax…...

When you are ready to begin concentrate on your breathing, take in a deep breath, breathe in through your nose. Take the breath deep into your body, breathe out through your mouth. Breathe in through your nose and out through your mouth, once more in through the nose and out through the mouth. Now still concentrating on your breathing begin to breathe naturally…...

You are sitting on a comfortable bench near to the edge of a lake. The sun is shining and even though it is only late March it feels warm upon your face and body. The water of the lake is crystal clear, and you can see small rocks and stones beneath the water. Look to your right. There is a path around the edge of the lake leading to some trees…...Get up from the bench and begin to walk along the path towards the trees. As you walk you have the lake on your left and on your right, there is a moss-covered dry-stone wall. The wall is covered in small ferns growing in the moss and amongst the stones and at the base of the wall primroses are in full bloom. Their delicate perfume fills the air…...You have reached the trees, continue to walk along this path…...The path is now beginning to lead you away from the lake. You decide to leave the path and walk amongst the trees back towards the lake. You tread carefully as tree roots are growing near to the surface of the soil. Look at the pattern of the large tree roots as they spread out above the ground. Now see smaller roots the further away they get from the tree....... Continue to walk to the lake shore......Now you are standing at the edge of the lake. Look down into the cool clear water. A fish swims idly by and small waves lap against an outcrop of rock. The only sounds are birdsong and the gentle lapping of the water. Take a deep breath, smell the earthy soil and the pine resin. Stay here for a while enjoying the peace and tranquillity of this place......Now begin to walk back amongst the trees to the path......Turn left and continue along the path. Look at the pine trees, their bark is deeply etched and grooved. The smell of pine resin fills the air......In front of you you can see that the path leads out of the trees, continue to walk towards the edge of the trees......You have now left the shade of the trees and have reached an open field, the grass runs down to the edge of the lake. Walk towards the water...... The bank of the lake is covered in native daffodils. Go and sit on the grass amongst the sea of bright yellow. Sit a while admiring the flowers their tiny heads nodding in the gentle breeze. The sun is warm on your back. You feel warm and contented and at peace......A family of ducks swims past, the tiny fluffy chicks swim behind their mother......Now stand and begin to walk back towards the trees, walk back along the path. The lake is now on your right and the moss-covered wall on your left. Reach out and stroke the soft gentle moss. As you look the moss is covered in tiny droplets of water, tiny insects hide in the forest of moss...... Continue your way. Now you can see the edge of the trees. Walk out of the trees and back to sit on the bench......

When you are ready to return slowly begin count down from five, move your shoulders and head from side to side as you come back to the room. If you lit a candle when you blow it out, send love and healing to those in need and take a moment to reflect upon the season. Take some small sips of water to ground yourself.

The inspiration for this meditation is the shore of Lake Windermere beginning just below Wray Castle. A few days after I had completed this meditation, we saw on the news that a great many of the trees had been devastated by storms Dudley and Eunice.

A SPRINGTIME WALK, LUSTLEIGH TO MORETON

Dozens, hundreds, thousands. Nay! Millions of primroses line the way,
Hedgerows, ditches, woodlands and boulder strewn fields and hillsides,
Pale yellow, delicate, sweetly perfumed,
Heads turned towards the bright spring sunshine and forget-me-not blue sky.

Newborn lambs stretch out in soft spring grass,
Ewes in labour lie panting under the trees,
Mums clean their newborn as they struggle to their feet,
They find their first drink of colostrum laden milk.

Newly planted hedgerows begin to show new bright green leaves emerging,
Blackthorn has flowers in abundance, a promise of sloes aplenty in the autumn,
Bright yellow daffodils line the verges,
Trumpets turned to face the sun.

Enormous bumble bees drone and buzz,
They search out tree blossom and dandelion heads laden with nectar,
Ladybirds crawl from leaf to stem,
Aphids for breakfast after a long winter slumber.

Everywhere new life emerging, as daylight hours grow, nights
become shorter,
The birds are beginning to herald each new dawn,
Their chorus becoming louder each day,
They protect their boundaries and call for a mate.

This day of warm bright spring sunshine brings promise of
summer to come,
Of days lazing in the cool shade of trees in full leaf,
Dibbling toes in cool clear streams,
Sharing picnics and fun and laughter with family and good
friends.

SWEET POTATO CURRY.
SERVES 2-3

1 large, sweet potato
1 onion
3 cloves of garlic
1 large carrot, grated
400g can of chickpeas
8 large tomatoes, skinned (if using fresh tomatoes add ½ teaspoon sugar) or a jar of tomato cooking sauce or a 400g can of chopped tomatoes
Tomato puree
1 heaped dessertspoon curry powder
1 heaped dessert spoon yeast flakes
1 heaped teaspoon turmeric
1 heaped teaspoon ground ginger
Vegetable stock cube
Ground black pepper
A little vegetable oil for frying

Peel and cut up the sweet potato into small cubes. Place into a medium sized saucepan and just cover with water. Cook for approximately 15 minutes until softened, drain.

Whilst the sweet potato is cooking peel and chop the onion and garlic, add to a large saucepan with a little oil, fry until softened. Chop the skinned tomatoes.

Now add all the spices and fry for one minute stirring constantly. Add the chopped tomatoes, a heaped tablespoon of tomato puree, stock cube, black pepper, chickpeas, plus at least half of the water from the can and the sweet potato. Stir well and simmer for around 40 minutes.

As stock cubes are fairly salty, I never add any salt until I have tasted the curry.

Serve with flatbreads.

FLATBREAD

200g plain flour
Pinch salt
2 tablespoons of vegetable oil
100 ml warm water

Place dry ingredients into a bowl. Add the oil and warm water, mix the dough together using your hands and knead until you have a smooth dough, this takes around 5 minutes. Either use immediately or cover with a damp cloth for half an hour. Divide into 4 pieces and roll out to around 1/8 inch thick. Cook in a hot pan, no oil is needed, for about 2 minutes a side. When cooked place on a plate and cover with a tea towel to keep warm and soft.

OSTARA SIMNEL CAKE

*1 mug of strong cold tea
2 mugs of mixed dried fruits of your choice
125g vegan margarine
2/3 mug of sugar. I use half soft brown and half granulated
2 mugs self-raising flour
1 heaped dessert spoon black treacle
1 heaped tablespoon chia seeds
1 teaspoon white wine vinegar
1 teaspoon baking powder
2 teaspoons of mixed spices of your choice

250g white marzipan, plus extra to decorate the top of the finished cake if you have a very sweet tooth!

2 tablespoons brandy, optional

8" round cake tin lined

Place the dried fruits into a bowl with the cold tea. Leave to soak for about 2 hours

Line your cake tin and roll out the marzipan to form a round that just fits inside the tin. Set to one side.

Pre heat the oven to 160oC

Combine all your dry ingredients in a mixing bowl. Gradually add the fruit and tea mixture taking care that the mix is even and not lumpy. Place half of the cake mix into your lined tin. Carefully place the rolled-out marzipan onto the cake mix. Add the rest of the cake mix to your baking tin.

Cook for about 50 minutes to an hour. Test with a skewer.

When cold prick the top of your cake and spoon over the brandy if using.

This keeps well for a week or so after cooking. I would make at least 24 hours before needed. It also freezes well.

* I use a 300ml capacity mug

CHOCOLATE BROWNIES

75g pitted dates
5 tablespoons boiling water
75g vegan margarine
150g sugar
200g plain flour
25g cocoa powder
2 tablespoons golden syrup
2 teaspoons baking powder
1 teaspoon vanilla essence
60g vegan dark chocolate, chopped
100ml vegan milk, I use oat milk

Line an 8" square brownie tin.

Put the dates into a bowl with the boiling water. Set aside for 20 minutes to soak. Blitz to a paste.
Place all the dry ingredients into a mixing bowl. Add the dates, vanilla essence and vegan milk. Mix well.

Oven 160oC for approximately 30 minutes. Cool in the tin. This cuts into 12 pieces if you are greedy or 18 if you aren't!

Enjoy on its own or with vegan cream or ice cream or custard.

BELTAINE

A VILLAGE TALE

*C*ome *my friends and greet the Summer, Beltaine is here once more. Maypole dancing, Morris dancing, see in the warmer summer days. Herald the new life all around, apple blossoms abound in our orchards, the promise of apples to store and cider to make. Hail and welcome!*

The orchard had been bustling with activity for several days. The Maypole had been raised and decorated with brightly coloured ribbons of red, white, green, and yellow. The colours of the season. The greens and yellows of nature and white and red to symbolise the purity of the Goddess and maidens and the force of lust and love of potential consorts and lovers. The union of male and female, for the maypole dance is a symbol of hope, joy, and fertility. An ancient phallic symbol, the maypole represents the masculine and the ribbons the feminine.

Oak and all the other children who lived in the village had been bought up to celebrate this special time of the year. The Queen of the May was crowned on her throne which was decorated with garlands of spring flowers. The throne itself sat upon the large slab of granite in the orchard and later in the year her name would be engraved in the hard almost unyielding stone.

The whole village looked forward to the Mayday celebrations and everyone who was able, joined in the preparations.

Demi and many of the other women in the village had, for many days, been busily baking cakes and pastries. Fin and

Oak had been busy helping to raise the Maypole itself and ensuring that the ribbons were securely attached so that none came loose during the dancing. Many years ago, the Maypole would be cut down fresh each year, usually a pine or birch tree, nowadays the village wanted to preserve their trees and so the pole was stored away to use year after year.

Finally, on the day before the Beltaine celebrations, the Altar was set up in the orchard ready to be decorated by Demi, Fin, and Oak before sunrise on Beltaine morning.

As the sun set on May Eve Demi and Fin walked around the orchard to check that all was ready for the following day.

"This all looks ready for tomorrow," said Demi.

"Yes, everyone has worked so hard over the past few days to ensure that we have a Beltaine to remember," agreed Fin. In the distance Demi and Fin could hear cries and shrieks of laughter from the woodlands above the village. It seemed that all the young, free and unmarried were out enjoying May Eve. Many couples had paired up for life on May Eve and there was usually a rash of weddings in June and July when relationships forged on May Eve were consummated.

"It sounds as though all of the young and free and easy are out 'Flower picking' on this fair evening," observed Demi.

"Yes, I hope that Oak is behaving himself," said Fin.

A few days before May Eve Fin and Demi had sat Oak down to explain that although May Eve had a fun and frivolous side it also had a serious side too.

"As you are now fifteen you are old enough to join in with all the Mayday festivities. You can go out into the woodlands on May Eve to join with friends and to have fun as have countless generations of young people in the village, but you need to take care," began Fin.

"Oh, Dad it's not a 'Birds and Bees' lecture, is it?"

As Oak had spent so much time observing nature, and going out with Richard the Vet on his rounds, he was well versed in the cycles of life. Demi continued, "No Oak it's not. What we mean is that one day you will be the Lord of the Wildwood and you need to save yourself for the right partner. The right person who will one day take on my role as Lady of the Land and Harvest. Go out and have fun, flirt, but as for anything further it stops at that. Do you understand?"

"Don't worry Mum and Dad, I will take care. Am I allowed to stay out all night like everyone else does though?"

"Yes, that is what we are saying, stay out and have fun. Please ensure that you are home at least an hour before dawn to get cleaned up and ready for the ceremony," said Demi.

"Will Dad be out too as Lord of the Wild woods?"

"Of course, however I will be keeping well out of your way," said Fin, "Now that you are older you need to be able to help us to lead the ceremonies. You are learning so much now, in a few years time we plan to leave the village so that you can take up your role as Guardian of the Village and Lord of the Wild Wood and Lord of the Wild Hunt."

Oak looked both shocked and pleased to think that in a few years he would take on the massive responsibility for the Village. The place where he was born and grown up. The special magical place where he had first seen the Fae as they danced at Midsummer in the Glade. The place where he had first seen a lamb born. He knew the woodlands and fields inside out now, but he also knew that he had so much more to learn.

"When were you planning to leave. Please say that it's not just yet," implored Oak.

"No, it won't be for a few years lad, don't worry, we shall still be here for a while yet to help and guide you on your special path in life," said Fin.

"Phew. I thought that you were planning to leave soon."

"No not just yet," said Demi. "Now scram, go and help set up the orchard. I need to get baking!" laughed Demi.

True to his word Oak arrived home an hour before

sunrise on May morning. He looked flushed and heavy eyed but after a quick shower seemed revived and ready to help lead the Beltaine ceremony. As Oak made his way to the orchard he could see that other young people, and some not so young, were wearily making their way home after a night in the woodlands and fields. When Oak reached the orchard, he could see that Demi and Fin were busily decorating the Altar.

"Ah, here you are, give me a hand with the Altar cloth," said Fin. Demi greeted her son with a hug.

"Yes please, can you help Dad with the cloth and then help me with the candles?" asked Demi. Soon the Altar was set. The cloth was beautifully hand woven in shades of greens, blues and yellows and looked splendid against the setting of the apple trees that were now in full bloom, pink and white blossoms adorned all the trees. The occasional petal floating gracefully to the ground. The hedgerows were covered in may blossom and everywhere seemed to be holding its breath in readiness for the beginnings of summer.

Soon everyone began to arrive for the ceremony and festivities. Sarah and Mike, Demi's parents made their way across the orchard to where Demi, Fin and Oak were waiting to begin the ceremony. Not for the first time, Demi thought that they were beginning to look their age. Sarah and Mike had moved to the village many years ago when Demi had agreed to become Fin's consort. They had been present at Oak's birth and had thrown themselves into village life with gusto. Now time was beginning to take its toll and Demi wondered how much longer they would be on the Earth.

"Mum, Dad, come and sit here near to the Altar," said Demi as she greeted Sarah and then Mike with a hug.

"Oh, we are fine and don't need a seat," replied Sarah. Demi looked at Fin who had guessed what Demi was thinking.

"Oh, we bought these chairs across especially for you," said Fin.

"And I decorated them with green and yellow cushions," said Oak.

"Well, I am feeling a little tired," said Mike, "A little sit down will do us good, it will be a long day. Come on Sarah, sit yourself down for a while." As Sarah and Mike sat down Fin winked at Demi over their heads. A little psychology always helped these days as Sarah and Mike began to get much frailer but trying desperately to hold onto their independence.

"Ah. Our Queen of the May has arrived," said Fin. Demi walked across the orchard to greet the Green Man and the May Queen and her flower attendants.

"Hello Molly how are you today?" asked Demi.

"OK miss, a bit nervous though."

"It's fine to be a little nervous, just concentrate on enjoying your special day," encouraged Demi. Molly smiled. "Now everyone line up and hold your flowers for a guard of honour. Then when your Queen of the May has walked through the guard of honour archway on the arm of the Green Man join in and walk behind her." Instructed Demi to the attendants.

"Yes miss," they chorused. Demi walked back to Fin and Oak.

"Are they ready to begin?" asked Fin. Demi nodded, "Yes, a little nervous but all ready."

Fin, Demi, and Oak raised their brightly decorated staffs aloft. Fin began, "Now we begin our ceremony to welcome the Spring by crowning our Queen of the May. Come forward Molly." Molly and the Green Man walked forward through the floral guard of honour towards where Demi, Fin and Oak stood. Everyone cheered and drummed as Molly and her attendants slowly walked towards the throne set high upon the stone slab. As Molly reached the stone Demi and the Green Man helped her to climb the steps and lead her to her throne where Oak was waiting with the crown of spring flowers. When Molly was seated Oak held the crown aloft for all to see.

"I now crown you as our Queen of the May. Today you shall reign over our village and all who you see now standing before you." Oak placed the crown upon Molly's head to loud cheering and applause and calls from the crowd.

"Enjoy your day!"

"Yes, your Majesty."

"Yes Ma'am," were some of the good-natured comments. Fin climbed onto the stone and raised his staff for quiet.

"Now our Queen of the May is crowned. Let us give thanks for our Village. For the new season. We give thanks to the elements of the Earth, Air, Fire and Water and of the Spirit of the special place that we all call our home. Let us hope that the Goddess blesses our fields and that the elements treat us kindly so our crops may grow strong and tall in readiness for our harvest in a few months time. Hail and welcome!"

"Hail and Welcome!"

"Now it is time for our Queen of the May and her attendants to lead the Maypole dancing. Away to the village green!" cried Demi. The Queen and her attendants led everyone towards the village green where the Morris dancers were waiting to strike up their music. Everyone gathered around the Maypole, the Queen, and her attendants, and many of the older village children. When all were ready Molly stepped forward.

"Is all ready for the Maypole dancing?"

"We are all ready," the dancers replied. "Then take up your ribbons ready for to dance!"

The music rang out and everyone took their assigned ribbon and began to dance. The dancers wove their way backwards and forwards ducking and passing between one another with much laughter and a few slips and trips until the whole length of the Maypole was covered in a multicoloured kaleidoscope of ribbons. Everyone fell to the ground laughing and giggling and trying to catch their breath before the second dance later in the day when the ribbons would be untangled once more.

Now the Morris dancers took their turn to dance, hindered, and helped, by the Green Man. The crowd clapped to the music, and some joined in with the dancers. The sounds of the clashing together of wooden staffs and ringing bells filled the air.

Demi, Fin and Oak helped to set out the May feast on the trestle tables that had been set up on the village green the day before. Already several of the villagers had been busily quaffing ale, cider and mead and needed a hefty slice of bread accompanied by a wedge of cheese to soak up some of the alcohol.

After the lunchtime feast the Maypole dancers performed the second dance of the day. This was a much more sedate affair as everyone had eaten far too much. Then came the running races, sack races, three legged races and egg and spoon races all were accompanied by much laughter. Several pairs in the three-legged races ended up in a giggling heap fortunately, without any injuries to mar the fun.

Dancing and singing continued well into the night. Many pairings disappeared into the woodlands and fields above the village. As Demi and Fin made their way home late into the evening Fin observed, "We shall be very busy with Handfastings come July and August."

"Yes, and by the looks of it, with baby naming ceremonies come February and March," smiled Demi.

BELTAINE WOODLAND WALK

Early morning dew sparkles on fresh green blades of grass,
Precious diamond gems of nature dazzle.

Muddy puddles strew the forest path, I stop to read the tracks,
Badger, fox, deer, fellow humans, and dogs have all passed this way.

Navelwort, ivy, and unfurling ferns grow from the exposed roots of an ancient tree,
Countless winter rains have lashed the soil eroding the hillside away.

New leaves uncurling on Hazel and Beech. Holly leaves shine bright in the early sunlight,
Bright red berries still glisten.

Lesser Celandines shine like a bright yellow beacon,
Blackberry bramble bushes, delicate new fresh leaves bring a promise of abundant fruit in Autumn.

Bluebell leaves spear the woodland floor, heralding an aromatic carpet of blue,
Pale yellow Primroses line our path.

Sunlight makes dappled patterns upon the woodland floor,
I glance upwards through tall branches as they reach for the brilliant blue sky.

New spring growth is all around us,
The promise of long warm summer days to come.

SPRING INTO SUMMER MEDITATION

Sit quietly where you won't be disturbed, take a drink to ground yourself when you return. Light a candle or some incense if appropriate, adjust your clothes and get comfortable......

Close your eyes and begin to relax......

When you are ready to begin concentrate on your breathing. Take in a deep breath, breathe in through your nose, take the breath deep into your body. Breathe out through your mouth, breathe in through your nose and out through your mouth, once more in through the nose and out through the mouth. Now still concentrating on your breathing begin to breathe naturally......

You are walking along a single-track tarmac lane. To either side there are high hedgerows filled with white star shaped flowers, bluebells, cow parsley and pink campion......You come to a gap in the hedge where there is a gate. Stop and lean on the gate, the field is full of ewes and their lambs, some are lying down basking in the sun, others are running in groups whilst the ewes call them back. Some of the lambs are busily butting the ewes as they want a feed......In the distance you can see the turquoise and blue sea, reflecting the blueness of the sky. Small white tipped waves meet the shoreline. Stay here a while enjoying the view and marvelling at the new life all around, the lambs in the fields and the flowers in the hedgerow......

Now begin to walk on down the road. Soon the road becomes a woodland path. To your right there is a river. All around there are trees, some in full leaf others just beginning to break the leaf buds. The beech trees look as though their branches and trunks are almost black against the vivid bright green of their new leaves. The Hawthorn is just beginning to come into flower......The air is filled with the noise of birdsong, stay here and listen to the birds sing as they greet this new day......Now continue along the path, in the river you see dippers foraging for their breakfast, grey and yellow plumage disappearing underwater to emerge a short distance away. There is a sudden flash of the orange and blue plumage of a Kingfisher as he looks for a place to perch.

As you continue walking you see several fallen branches and rotten trees covered in coins, these are wishing trees where many make offerings to the Goddess and the God. Stay and place your own coin into the bark of a tree......Continue along the riverbank, the sunlight glistens on the water as it glides over small rocks and boulders. In the distance you hear the waterfall......The pathway is lined with ferns, primroses, and bluebells. As you get nearer to the waterfall many of the trees are adorned with ribbons. Stacks of small stones have been made as offerings to the Spirits of this place...... As you round the final bend you see the waterfall in all of its glory, stand in quiet contemplation......do you want to make your own offering? Bend and put your hands in the water, feel how cold it is. Scoop some water into your hands and wash your face. Feel the energy of the water, give thanks for the water...... When you feel that you are ready to leave this sacred space, begin to walk back the way you came, along the riverside path. The birds are almost silent now, as you walk back through the woodland......When you leave the wood retrace your footsteps along the tarmac lane and back past the field with the ewes and their lambs.

When you are ready to return slowly begin count down from five, move your shoulders and head from side to side as you come back to the room. If you lit a candle when you blow it out send love and healing to those in need and take a moment to reflect upon the season. Take some small sips of water to ground yourself.

The setting for this meditation is the wonderful St Nectan's Glen and waterfall

MUSHROOM AND WILD GARLIC RISOTTO, SERVES 3 OR 4

1 mug arborio rice
1 onion finely chopped
3 cloves garlic peeled, crushed and chopped
150g chestnut mushrooms
100g frozen peas
Large handful wild garlic or fresh spinach roughly chopped or torn
1 vegetable stock cube
Vegetable oil for frying
White wine, optional
Yeast flakes
Black pepper
Salt if needed
Boiling water

In a large pan fry the onion and garlic in a small amount of oil until opaque. Add the rice and stir for about a minute. Add about 1/3 of a mug of wine, if using, to your mug now top up with boiling water, add to the pan plus one more mug of boiling water and the stock cube. Cover and simmer for 10 minutes. Then stir in the peas. Cook for a further 5 minutes. At this stage you may need to add a small amount of water.
Wipe and slice the mushrooms. Add a small amount of oil to a frying pan.
Cook the mushrooms on a high heat until browned. Stir the mushrooms, yeast flakes and wild garlic into the rice mix, add a good amount of freshly ground black pepper.

I find that this makes enough for a good portion each for

two adults plus some leftovers to serve as a rice salad. I stir in about a dessertspoon of French dressing into the leftovers and store in the fridge to use the following day.

Instead of mushrooms you can use sun dried tomatoes, one of our favourites. I use about 100g chopped sun dried tomatoes, which is about a third of a large jar.

Note. I decided years ago that to make a traditional risotto by adding a small amount of liquid every few minutes is far too time consuming. I add all the liquid at the beginning and just stir the mix a couple of times during cooking. This thickens the mix just as well. Purists always add cream or butter just before serving. I never eat cream or butter, vegan or otherwise but there is nothing stopping you adding some if you so wish.

HUMMUS

1 400g can of chickpeas, drained. Reserve the liquid
1 heaped tablespoon tahini *
1 clove of garlic, crushed, optional
1 tablespoon lemon juice
Salt
White pepper or paprika

Place all the ingredients into a blender or food processor. Blitz until a smooth paste. If the mix is a little thick add 1 or 2 tablespoons of the chickpea water.

Hummus is so versatile. It is great for serving with batons of carrot, cucumber, and pepper to use as a dip.
We use it for sandwiches and on toast.

For a summer mezze picnic served with flatbreads, green salad, sundried tomatoes, and olives plus a bottle of something chilled either non-alcoholic or wine of your choice.

* Tahini contains sesame seeds, which some are allergic to. Tahini freezes well. I usually use an ice cube tray to freeze, then to save food wastage, only defrost the amount I need.

SALAD DRESSING

Rapeseed or olive oil
White wine vinegar
1 heaped teaspoon of Dijon or wholegrain mustard
½ teaspoon of sugar

I use 2/3 oil to 1/3 vinegar. Place all the ingredients in a jar. Screw on the lid and shake well. Decant into a dressing bottle or leave the mix in the jar and spoon out. Store in the fridge and use within two weeks.

FLAPJACKS

250g sugar, white or brown
250g vegan margarine
2 rounded dessertspoons golden syrup
360g oats
2 teaspoons ground ginger
2 tablespoons plain flour.

Line an 8" x 12" cake tin with baking parchment, ensure there is enough paper to hold onto when you need to remove the flapjack from the tin.

Put the sugar, margarine and golden syrup into a saucepan and melt slowly until the ingredients are combined. Add the oats, flour and ground ginger to the pan. Stir well. Turn into the cake tin.

Oven 160oc for approximately 30 minutes. Leave to cool for five minutes then carefully score into 18 pieces. Leave in the tin to cool and then gently lift out of the tin by the lining paper and cut into 18 pieces.

I have always had problems making flapjacks. For years I struggled to get them to hold together without falling apart and removing the cooked flapjacks from the tin. I found by trial and error that the flour helps to bind the mix and then to use the lining paper to remove the cooked flapjack so that I could cut it up into proper pieces instead of a mass of crumbs.

SUMMER
SOLSTICE
A VILLAGE TALE

T   *he shortest night, the longest day. For a few days Our Sun God*
stands still in the sky, it is time to welcome the summer. At this
time, at summer's height, we revel in the long daylight hours. Soon the days
will begin to shorten once again. A time for goodbyes and a time of welcome.
Crops are ripening in the fields; it is a time to holiday before the toil of the
autumn harvests begins.

The Summer Solstice, as is often the case, dawned misty and murky with a real chill in the air. Demi and Fin had been up and about since before daylight to prepare for the ceremony to welcome the sunrise on the longest day of the year and the battle between the Oak and Holly Kings.

Oak had been keeping vigil overnight, with many others from the village, they had watched the sun set and they would break their vigil only when the sun rose at the Solstice dawn.

Now that Oak was eighteen and adult he had been chosen to fight in the battle between the Oak and Holly Kings that had taken place at the Winter Solstice ceremony. Now he would be fighting in the Summer Solstice ceremony, his crown would be forfeit.

Oak stood up and yawned and stretched. He walked to the hedge that lined the orchard and running his hands through the leaves that were wet with the early morning dew wiped his face with the cold reviving water. Many of those present followed his lead.

"Brr, a chilly start to the day, but it promises to be fine later. Look at the sky, the cloud is beginning to thin out and there is a touch of blue beginning to appear," said Raven, a close friend of Oak's who had been chosen to be the Holly king for the battle.

"Yes, it promises to be a fine day. Just right for me to thrash you in the battle!" joked Oak. Of course, Oak knew that as the King of the Summer he would be beaten by the Holly King, and he would be losing his crown to Raven.

Oak led the way to the very top of the orchard where the horizon was visible and where the very tip of the rising sun could be seen. Down below in the orchard he could see Demi and Fin putting the final touches to the Altar. Those who had chosen to attend the ceremony were beginning to assemble. The sunrise could be viewed from the top of the hill above the orchard a few minutes earlier than at the bottom of the hill in the orchard.

The sky began to clear and change colour from milky white to a very pale blue and then a deeper blue shot through with fingers of pale oranges and reds. Then suddenly the sun began to pierce the horizon it's red and orange tip soon began to grow into a half moon shape. Oak led the group back down the hill to take their places within the circle.

Fin raised his hands for silence. "We greet this new dawn, this new day. We give thanks for the Solstice Sunrise. We give thanks for this blessed time of the year, long days, and short nights. A time when the Sun God strides across the skies from early in the morning until late in the evening. We give thanks for our family and good friends. We give thanks to the Goddess and the God for all the natural world and all the life around us. Blessed Be."

"Blessed Be."

Demi was standing in her place next to Fin and Oak stood beside her. Demi's eyes were full of tears. Her beloved parents Sarah and Mike were not at the ceremony. They were now of a great age and too frail to attend. Demi wondered how much longer it would be before they made the great journey across the Bridge to the Summerlands beyond.

Demi was dreading the time when her parents were no longer there. They were a huge part of her life, and a huge part of Fin and Oak's lives. They were much valued members of village life and would be missed by everyone. Demi also knew that the time when Demi and Fin were to leave the Village was rapidly drawing closer. They had not made any announcement yet or spoken to Oak, but Demi and Fin had discussed their departure privately and had decided that the time would be very soon. Oak was eighteen, adult and in a very few years would be able to take on the role of Lord of the Wildwood and Lord of the Wildhunt.

Demi realised that the ceremony was almost over.

"We give thanks to the Guardians of the North, West, South and East and the Spirit of this special place. Hail and Farewell."

"Hail and Farewell."

"This ceremony is now over. The circle may be broken. Now is the time for the battle of the Oak and Holly Kings."

As everyone was moving to the open space at the bottom of the orchard where the battle was to take place Demi had a feeling of dread in her stomach. "I need to go to see Mum and Dad," she whispered to Fin. Fin could see by the look on Demi's face that she feared that the worst had happened, and that Sarah and Mike were breathing their last.

"I will come with you. I can't let you go alone."

"No Oak is fighting, and you need to oversee the battle and the crowning. Come later." Fin gave Demi a hug before she ran out of the orchard towards Sarah and Mike's cottage. As she ran Demi thought of Fin, his parents, Sweetbriar and Beech had also passed at this time of the year.

As Demi neared the cottage her worst fears were realised, Kate, the carer opened the front door.

"Quickly, off you go up the stairs," said Kate. Demi rushed to the bedroom, the curtains were still drawn. Sarah and Mike were lying on the bed hand in hand.

"We knew that you would know when our time was here. We knew that you would come just in time," smiled Mike.

"Open the curtains, let in the Summer Solstice sun so that we may feast our eyes upon it one last time," said Sarah. Demi opened the curtains as wide as they would go. Sarah and Mike lay watching the sun as it rose in the sky and flooded the room with a pure brilliant light. Demi sat next to them waiting, holding Sarah's hand. Soon the sun had risen above the window. Kate stood in the doorway opposite to wait with Demi. With a final smile and a squeeze of Demi's hand Sarah and Mike closed their eyes for the last time just as Fin arrived. He took Demi in his arms and held her for a very long time as the tears flowed. At last, she settled, "OK now?" asked Fin.

"Yes," said Demi trying to smile and to clean up her face. "I'll just pop and wash my face, I will be back soon."

"Thank you, Kate, for being here with Demi," said Fin.

"My pleasure. I knew that you couldn't come as it was the Solstice. I will call the undertaker for you and begin to tidy up Sarah and Mike ready for their final journey. All of you have done so much for the Village over the years. It was the least I could do."

They heard a noise downstairs; Oak took the stairs two at a time.

"Sorry son you are too late," said Fin.

"Where is mum?"

"Here, I have just been to wash my face. I am OK'ish now," Demi gave Oak a hug.

"Oh mum, I'm so sorry I wasn't here."

"It's OK. Kate was with me and then dad arrived just after gran and grandad had passed." Demi turned to Kate. "Let me help you wash them and to tidy their hair."

"If, you are sure?"

"Yes, I am sure." Demi turned to Fin and Oak, "Please can you go and tell everyone the news. Please say that we want today to continue as it should, I want everyone to drink a toast to mum and dad and to enjoy the feast. Make it a wake in their honour, I will join you later after Kate and I have done last offices and the undertaker has been."

After a hug for Fin and Oak they left the cottage to let everyone know the news about Sarah and Mike.

As Fin and Oak approached the orchard a silence fell, and the Morris dancers became quiet. Fin and Oak climbed onto the top of the large stone slab, "We are sorry to announce that Sarah and Mike have just passed from this world into the next world beyond the Bridge."

Everyone was saddened to hear the news, and some made to leave the orchard to go home.

"Please stay," called Fin. "Demi has asked me to tell you that she wants the day to continue as it usually would. When we hold our feast in a short while she would like a toast raised in Sarah and Mike's memory. Sarah and Mike made this village their home many years ago, they loved the ceremonies and the traditions. They would want you to enjoy today and to celebrate as usual. Now Morris dancers, play your music!"

Much to everyone's surprise the day did carry on much as usual. A toast was raised by Fin and Demi at the feast and the dancing went on until sunset.

A few days later a funeral ceremony was held in the orchard. The Altar and coffins were decked with flowers as everyone wanted to place a flower to remember Sarah and Mike.

Almost everyone who lived in the village came to honour Sarah and Mike. Fin and Demi stood in the centre of the circle next to the coffins. At the points of the circle that represented the four elements of Air, Fire, Water and Earth stood Sarah and Mike's oldest friends who would call in the Guardians. Oak stood to one side.

Fin raised his arms in the air for silence.

"Today we meet to say Hail and Farewell to two of our dearest friends, Sarah and Mike. They have lived in the Village for many years, they moved here when Demi agreed to become my Consort many, many years ago. Now it is their time to leave this special place that they loved to call home. Now I ask Demi to cast a circle." Demi began to walk around the orchard to cast a sacred space using her staff, whilst she walked Oak played his drum, gentle drumbeats at first then as Demi completed the circle the sound became louder ending with a great bang. Demi took her place inside the circle at Fin's side.

"Now I ask those chosen, to call in the Guardians, beginning with the East," said Fin. Everyone turned to face the eastern quarter of the circle.

"Guardian of the East, we welcome you today. Element of Air may the Spirits of Sarah and Mike be carried to their rest by your gentle breezes. Hail and Welcome."

"Hail and Welcome."

Now everyone turned to face the southern quarter of the circle.

"Guardian of the South. We welcome you today. Element of Fire. Fire that warmed Sarah and Mike during long cold winter days. The fire of the Sun that warms us and cheers us. Hail and Welcome."

"Hail and Welcome."

Then everyone turned to the western quarter. "Guardian of the West. Element of Water. Pure clear water that flows through our sacred Glade and orchard. Pure clear water that sustained Sarah and Mike throughout their lives. Hail and Welcome."

"Hail and Welcome."

Finally, everyone turned to the north. "Guardian of the North. Element of Earth. The Earth that is our home. The very Earth that we walk upon. The Earth that brings forth our crops from the seeds that we sow, crops that fed and sustained Sarah and Mike throughout their lives. Hail and Welcome."

"Hail and Welcome."

Oak stepped forward to stand before the two flower decorated coffins. "Today we are gathered here to say farewell to my grandparents, Sarah, and Mike. Sarah and Mike were friends to all who knew them, they helped everyone in the Village. They helped to prepare the orchard and Altars for our ceremonies. They helped those less fortunate than themselves. Above all they were a great help and support to my parents, Demi and Fin and they have been a constant part of my life. We wish them a safe journey to their next lives, their next great adventure together. At Samhain their souls will be led from the village to finally depart from this place they loved so much. They will always have a special place in our hearts and always be remembered. Blessed Be."

"Blessed Be."

Now Demi stepped forward, "Today we have honoured and remembered Sarah and Mike, my beloved parents. I thank you all for coming today to wish them well on their final journey. I thank all of you for your friendship and love over the past years and for all your good wishes and support over the past few days. Now we give thanks to the Guardians before the procession up the hill to the cemetery where we shall lay them to rest in the arms of the Goddess."

Fin stepped forward. "Please can we thank the Guardians. Beginning with the north." Everyone turned to face the northern quarter.

"Guardians of the North. We give thanks for your presence here today. Guardian of the Earth, we ask that the bodies of Sarah and Mike lie in your arms for all eternity. Hail and Farewell."

"Hail and Farewell."

Everyone turned to face the west. "Guardian of the West we give thanks for your presence here today. May your gentle waters encourage grasses and flowers to grow over the last resting place of Sarah and Mike. Hail and Farewell."

"Hail and Farewell."

Now everyone turned to face the south. "Guardian of the South. Element of fire may the sun warm the ground as we sow seeds upon the final resting place of Sarah and Mike. Hail and

Farewell." *"Hail and Farewell."*

Finally, everyone turned to face the east. "Guardian of the East. Guardian of the element of Air, may your gentle breezes scatter the wildflower seeds that we sow far and wide so that their beauty may be enjoyed by all. Hail and Farewell."

"Hail and Farewell."

Fin held his staff in the air for quiet. "This part of our ceremony is now over; the circle may be broken. Those who wish follow us up the hill to the cemetery please can you help to gather up the flowers so we may place them around the graves."

The procession made its way slowly up the hill. They reached the final resting place that Demi had chosen for Sarah and Mike, gently and reverently the coffins were lowered into the earth. Demi picked up a handful of earth and cast it into the grave. "May you rest in peace; may the seasons come and go. May the flower seeds that we shall cast over the bare earth grow to be a small wildflower meadow to nurture our Bees and other pollinators. May the birds of the air enjoy the seeds as they blow on the breeze. May gentle rains water the earth, Blessed Be."

"Blessed Be."

Fin and Oak in their turn threw handfuls of earth into the grave before the keeper of the cemetery began to fill in the grave. Except for Demi, Fin, and Oak everyone returned to the orchard for tea and cake or a glass or two of something stronger to reminisce. When the earth was finally all replaced Demi, Fin and Oak liberally scattered the grave with wildflower seeds.

Oak gave a final blessing, "May the Goddess bless you and may the Goddess keep you. Until we meet again across the Bridge in the Summerlands beyond." As the sun began to set it cast long shadows across the land as Demi, Fin and Oak began to walk back towards the village arm in arm.

SUMMER SOLSTICE

The Mighty Oak and Holly Kings at the Solstices do battle,

Light green coronet versus a crown of dark glossy thorns,

Shiny brown acorns delight Autumn days,

Glistening red berries shine in deep midwinter,

In woodland glades throughout the land,

Battles rage at Midsummer and Midwinter,

To and fro the combatants fight,

Swords clash, steel upon steel as sparks fly high,

To the victor the spoils, the prize to reign half of the year,

Crowns are surrendered to the Lord of the Wildwood,

To safely keep until the next Solstice Sunrise.

SUMMER SOLSTICE MEDITATION

Sit quietly where you won't be disturbed, take a drink to ground yourself when you return. Light a candle or some incense if appropriate, adjust your clothes and get comfortable……
Close your eyes and begin to relax……

When you are ready to begin concentrate on your breathing. Take in a deep breath, breathe in through your nose, take the breath deep into your body. Breathe out through your mouth, breathe in through your nose and out through your mouth, once more in through the nose and out through the mouth. Now still concentrating on your breathing begin to breathe naturally……

You are sitting on a bench in a walled garden, it is midsummer. The sun is shining warmly from a cloudless blue sky. You can hear the gentle splash of water from a fountain in a nearby pond. You are surrounded by roses of shades of pink and peach, their sweet scent drifts towards you on the gentle summer breeze…....
You decide to explore the garden, stand up and turn to your left. Walk towards the pond where the fountain is gently splashing as it falls onto the water. Stop at the pond, fish are darting amongst the soft fronds of water weed, shades of orange and gold dart between the weed and the fish almost seem to play around the fountain where the water lands…....Now continue to follow the path around the garden. You reach a border full of herbs, reach out and rub the leaves of the lavender, its sweet scent fills the air. The scent of the lavender makes you feel relaxed, sit on the wall that borders the herb garden. As you sit quietly you see that the lavender is covered in bees gently

moving from flower to flower as they collect pollen, their backs and legs are so laden you wonder how they can possibly fly......A small movement catches your eye, a tiny lizard has crept out of its hiding place between the stones of the wall and is now sunning itself. The sun reflects on his smooth burnished copper coloured skin......Now continue your way, you pass a border filled with bright yellow sunflowers, once again the flowers are covered in bees. Walk to the gate set into the wall of the garden. The arch surrounding the gate is covered in a sweetly scented climbing rose, look through the fret work on the top half of the gate towards the wildflower meadow beyond. Open the gate and walk towards the meadow......There is tree near the path, go and sit under the tree. Sit for a while and admire the flowers, pink campion, yellow rattle, blue cornflower, red field poppies, ox-eye daisies, corn cockle, knapweed and field marigold all growing amongst the gently swaying grasses. The field is covered in bees, butterflies, hover flies and numerous other flying insects all enjoying the warm sun and pollen......When you feel ready, stand slowly, and walk back towards the garden gate. Walk back around the garden to the bench and sit once more in the warm summer sun......

When you are ready to return, slowly begin count down from five, move your shoulders and head from side to side as you come back to the room. If you lit a candle when you blow it out send love and healing to those in need and take a moment to reflect upon the season. Take some small sips of water to ground yourself.

SAVOURY TARTS

1 pack ready rolled vegan puff pastry
8 large sun-dried tomatoes
400g cherry tomatoes
1 tablespoon olive oil
1 teaspoon balsamic vinegar
½ teaspoon sugar.

Cut the pastry into four rectangles. Score around the edges of each piece of pastry about ½ inch from the edge. Place onto lined baking sheets.
Blitz the sun-dried tomatoes into a smooth paste and spread over the base of the tarts. Cut the cherry tomatoes in half and arrange cut side down onto the tarts. Mix the oil, (I use the oil from the sun-dried tomato jar) balsamic and sugar to make a dressing and drizzle over the tarts.
Bake 200oC for 20 – 25 minutes.

Variations.

Instead of using all tomatoes use a mix of tomatoes and sliced mushrooms and sprinkle with some grated vegan cheese or vegan feta type cheese cut into small cubes.

If you want some smaller tarts cut the pasty into eight pieces.

Serve with a green salad. These are also nice for a picnic or lunch box.

SCONES

225g strong white bread flour
225g self-raising flour
5 teaspoons baking powder
100g vegan margarine
50g sugar
100g sultanas, optional
300ml vegan milk. I use oat milk.

Place the flour, baking powder and margarine into a bowl. Rub in the flour and fat until the mix looks like fine breadcrumbs.
Add the sugar and sultanas, if using. Stir well.
Add the milk and form into a soft dough.
Tip out the dough onto a floured worktop and flatten to about 3/4" thick. Flour a round pastry cutter and cut the dough into 12.
Place onto a lined baking sheet so that the scones are just touching, this helps the scones to rise. Brush with a little milk if desired and bake 200oC for about 15 minutes. Check the scones after 10 minutes. When cooked the scones should sound hollow when tapped on the base.

Serve with jam and vegan cream. I won't get into the argument which way round the jam and cream should be applied!

Variation.

Savoury scones

Replace the sultanas and sugar with 100g grated vegan cheese and 1 heaped tablespoon of yeast flakes.
Grate a little more cheese to sprinkle over the scones after they

have been placed onto the baking sheet.

These are lovely with soup or cheese and pickle or spread with vegan soft cheese or on their own

GENERIC JAM RECIPE

1 kg fruit of your choice
1.4kg sugar
3 tablespoons or 15 ml fresh lemon juice
½ bottle of Certo
1 teaspoon vegan margarine. If you are not vegan use a small cube of butter.

Jars with lids
Baking parchment or round jam pot covers
Small plate, place in the fridge about an hour before.

Pick over and wash your fruit. Place it into a large pan with the sugar and lemon juice. Cook slowly until all the fruit is pulpy. If you are making strawberry jam chop the strawberries first. I find if I replace some of the strawberries with blackcurrants it helps the jam to set.

When all the fruit is cooked add the butter or margarine. Slowly bring to a full rolling boil. Boil for around four minutes. Remove the jam from the heat and add the Certo. Try a tiny drop of the jam onto the cold plate it should crinkle if it is setting. If the jam is not setting boil again rapidly for around three minutes.

Pot up into your sterilised jam jars, cover with the jam pot covers, if you can't get the pot covers make your own by cutting rounds to fit the tops of your jars from baking parchment, and then put on the lids. When cold label and store in a cool dark place.

I always make two lots of jam to ensure I use up all the Certo.

This recipe is also useful if you find you have odd bits of fruit in the bottom of your freezer you need to use up.

LUGHNASADH

A VILLAGE TALE

T he feast of Lugh, we celebrate first harvest in all its glory. Golden fields of wheat, barley and oats shimmer and dance in the bright summer sun. We cut down the final sheaves and spill the blood of the Corn God upon the land. Our Lady raises and heals the God so he may return to us once more to lead the Wildhunt at Samhain.

"The Corn King is here, his sacrifice to bear,
With scythes and knives, we shall cut him down,
His blood to spill upon the Earth, her fertility to restore,
Up again he shall be raised to live again once more"

The Corn God bowed his head, his curling mop of shoulder length dark brown hair covered his face. The three men approached, the three reapers. "Are you ready to be slain, for your blood to be spilt upon the land. For your blood to return fertility to the soil so that we may have an abundant harvest in the coming year?" the Corn God nodded. One of the reapers ripped the shirt from the Corn God, the three reapers bound his hands and led him towards the middle of the field where the last stand of wheat had been left ready for the ceremony. The drumming and chanting stopped, and everyone looked across to where the reapers stood. The lead reaper, the spokesman, raised his scythe above his head, it glittered and gleamed in the bright July sun. The other two reapers gripped the God's hair and as they pulled his head back to expose his throat the lead reaper bought his scythe down and cut the throat of the God. Blood gushed and spurted from the fatal wound, a look of horror and recognition dawned upon the faces of the crowd and a shocked cries rang out around the field......

"And so, we are all agreed that this is the time, the best way forward?" asked Fin. Demi and Oak nodded, "Yes, it is time," agreed Demi. "It is time that we left the Village in the safe hands of Oak. Oak, you are now twenty-four, you are of age. You are sensible. We have all guided you well over the years, all of us. Fin and I, the craftsmen of the village, everyone has helped you to be the capable person that you have become."

Oak nodded again, "Yes, you were both around my age when you began to stop ageing, when the magick happened, I think?"

"Yes son, I was your age when I was first slain as the Corn God. Your Mother was the same age when she fulfilled her destiny as the Lady of the Land and Harvest and raised me up for the first time at the Lughnasadh ceremony after I had been slain. Then, with Sarah and Mike's blessing, she agreed to become my consort and to live here with me so that we could protect and look over the Village. This special place that we call home."

"It is a massive responsibility, but I knew that it was my destiny to take on the role. When are we going to announce our decision to the rest of the village, those who rely on us for help, those in their later years who have only known Dad as the Lord of the Wildwood and Corn God and Lord of the Wildhunt?"

Fin spoke, "I am sure that many will be expecting it. The older folks know that twenty-four is the usual age for the old Lord to hand over responsibility. For the new Lord to be crowned. They have seen you, over the past six years or so, take on more and more roles in ceremonies, to grow and mature into the wise man that you are now."

"I feel ready to take over," agreed Oak.

"Don't forget that we shall only be over in the next valley, we shall still be coming to the ceremonies. We shall be able to help and guide you if you need it, the time has come for you to take the lead as you see fit," continued Demi.

"It will be very lonely in the cottage without you,"

"One day soon you will find that 'Special' someone to help you with your work. She will come very soon of that I am certain," said Demi. "You will grow and work together and when the time is right you will be the parents of the next Lord and so it shall continue, Goddess willing."

Lughnasadh dawned clear and bright, and everyone was up and about early. Fresh bread was baked, and cider and red wine was made ready. Long trestle tables were set up around the edge of the last wheat field to be harvested. Chutneys, pickles, and ripe cheeses where all placed ready for the celebration lunch.

By late morning everyone had assembled in a circle ready for the ceremony. Drums began to beat as people began to dance and weave around the circle, then the harvest chant began.

"The Corn King is here, his sacrifice to bear,
With scythes and knives, we shall cut him down,
His blood to spill upon the Earth, her fertility to restore,
Up again he shall be raised to live again once more"

Then as the reapers with the bound Corn God approached silence fell, the reapers dragged the Corn God into the centre of the circle and stood with him next to the last sheaf to be harvested. The lead reaper raised his scythe and cut the exposed neck of the Corn God.

A cry of dismay rose from the crowd as they realised that the corn God was Oak and not Fin as they had been expecting. Fin walked to the centre of the circle with Demi at his side, "See the new Corn God is before you, he will now be raised up to live and to be made whole once again by the Lady of the Land and Harvest."

Demi stepped forward and placing her hands in Oak's now free and bloodied hands raised him up to his feet. "The corn God now lives. He will return at Samhain to lead the Wildhunt," this as Oak was led away by some of the elder ladies of the village.

Demi turned to face the crowd, "It is time for us to leave the Village. Time for us to relinquish responsibility to our son, Oak. Today I raised him up after he had been slain as the Corn God, the magick has now begun. Now he will no longer age until he chooses to leave the Village, soon he will find his lifelong companion."

"I am sure that our decision has come as no surprise to some of you," continued Fin. "Oak is now twenty-four, that is the traditional age when the new Lord of the Wildwood begins his stewardship. We shall remain in the village until Samhain and then as the Wildhunt ends Demi and I will lead the Souls from the village as we make our way to our new home. We shall return to visit; we shall return for the ceremonies. We shall return to lead the Handfasting ceremony of Oak and his chosen companion when the time comes."

The crowd cheered. Yes of course the time was right, the time had come. New blood would take over, new ideas would mingle with the old traditions as they always had. Demi raised her hands for quiet.

"Of course, Goddess willing, we shall also lead the naming ceremony for our grandson in the fullness of time. You haven't seen the last of us." Everyone laughed and cheered. "Now it is time for you all to break bread and to sprinkle an offering upon the Land to the Goddess. It is time for you to drink and to pour a libation onto the Land to honour the Corn God," continued Demi.

Bread and wine or cider was distributed to all, even the youngest. Everyone made their offerings to ensure a fine harvest for the following year, the Morris dancers struck a cord and everyone began to dance and sing.

After the Lughnasadh feast tables were cleared away, some of the children made corn dollies from the last sheaf of wheat to be harvested. They would take them home to hang above the door or mantlepiece of their homes in memory of the spirit of the Corn God and to give thanks to Mother Earth for the abundant harvest. Afterwards it was time for the running races, these became rather raucous as some of the adults who had consumed far too much cider insisted on joining in. Much laughter ensued as people tried to untangle from the heaps of twisted arms and legs.

Finally, it was time for harvest tea, sandwiches and cakes appeared from nowhere as if by magic. Yet more cider was consumed. Finally, it was time to begin the journey back down the hill to the village and home. Some of the younger children had already fallen asleep and had to be carried, some of the older folks who had fallen asleep in the fields slept under the hedge to wake the following morning covered in dew and with very sore heads.

BLACKBERRIES

Scrumptious, succulent, luscious, sweet and juicy,
Hedgerows loaded with gleaming black berries,
Birds and mammals forage, us humans too,
We try as we pick, sweet sticky juice runs down our chins,
Hands-stained purple, sometimes clothes too,
Blackberry harvesting rules we apply,
Never pick below the waist or above shoulder height,
Home, we go, cordials and jam to make,
Home-made wine in the demijohn bubbles and glugs,
Soon it will be time to sample last season's vintage,
Blackberries! Scrumptious, succulent, luscious, sweet and juicy.

BARAFUNDEL BAY
MEDITATION (SENSES
AND ELEMENTS)

S it quietly where you won't be disturbed, take a drink to ground yourself when you return. Light a candle or some incense if appropriate, adjust your clothes and get comfortable......
Close your eyes and begin to relax......

When you are ready to begin concentrate on your breathing, take in a deep breath, breathe in through your nose. Take the breath deep into your body, breathe out through your mouth. Breathe in through your nose and out through your mouth, once more in through the nose and out through the mouth. Now still concentrating on your breathing begin to breathe naturally......

You are standing barefoot on the seashore; waves are gently lapping around your feet and as you look down you see the sand shifting between your toes. As the waves flow in and out they reveal tiny pieces of shell that sparkle in the sunlight, colours of pink, orange and soft pearl glisten as the waves ebb and flow, ebb and flow, ebb and flow...... Watch the waves as they gently lap around your feet and toes......Now begin to walk along the beach, the sand feels warm, soft and grainy beneath your feet...... As you walk you see a rocky headland, begin to walk towards it......
When you reach the base of the headland you see a path that leads upwards towards the top of the cliff, put on your shoes, and begin to walk along the grassy path. The grass is very short and springy, everywhere there are wildflowers. Bird's foot trefoil, bright yellow against the green of the grass, harebells,

their blue heads nod in the gentle breeze. creeping thymes, tiny purple flowers adorn the grass.….. To your left is a hedge of gorse and broom, it is alive with sounds of bees as they hover from flower to flower to harvest nectar. Continue along the gently sloping path towards the top of the cliff.….. Now you have reached the top of the cliff pause and look at the view, the sea is a soft blue, you can see darker patches of blue as clouds overhead are reflected in the water. You see white topped waves and marker buoys in the bay. Now look down towards the base of the cliffs below, if you look very carefully you will see seals swimming and diving around the rocks. The waves are more powerful here, they send white spray up into the air before it crashes back into the sea, you can taste the salty tang in the air. Stand and watch the seals, listen to the sound of the waves……

Now continue to walk around the top of the cliff, enjoy the warm sunshine on your back, neck, and shoulders, feel how any tension is eased away……Gulls fly overhead, brilliant white against the blue of the sky……Now you have reached the far side of the cliff and the path begins to slope downwards, continue down the path. Breathe in the scents of the broom and wild thyme. As you walk you can hear the seed pods on the broom bursting and popping scattering seeds far and wide. Towards the base of the cliff the path takes you through a small wood, the area is covered in soft green ferns and the dark green leaves and light green bracts of navelwort adorn the mossy bark of the trees. Shafts of sunlight pierce the woodland, enjoy the earthy damp smell of the woods…… In the distance you can see the edge of the wood, walk towards the light. Now as you leave the wood behind you follow a sandy path towards a large freshwater lake, you see a bridge. Step onto the bridge and begin to walk across the bridge, as you cross the bridge look down into the fresh clear water. The lake is full of hundreds of fish, watch the fish as they swim idly through the weed, occasionally a fish will break the surface of the water making small ripples as they dive back down into the lake. You come to the end of the bridge, turn left and head along the sandy path back towards the beach. When you reach the beach remove your shoes, once again feel the softness of the sand between your toes as you walk across the beach to the edge of the sea. Stand once more in the shallow water, feel the gentle waves lap around your feet. See the tiny pieces of shell glistening in the sunlight. Give thanks to the element of the pure air, give thanks for the element and gift of water. Give thanks to the element of fiery sun, give thanks to the element of the earth. Lastly give thanks to the Spirit of this beautiful place.

When you are ready to return slowly begin count down from five. Move your shoulders and head from side to side as you come back to the room. If you lit a candle when you blow it out send love and healing to those in need and take a moment to reflect upon the elements. Take some small sips of water to ground yourself.

MEDITATION FOR LUGHNASADH. FIELDS OF GOLD

S it quietly where you won't be disturbed, take a drink to ground yourself when you return. Light a candle or some incense if appropriate, adjust your clothes and get comfortable......

Close your eyes and begin to relax......

When you are ready to begin concentrate on your breathing, take in a deep breath, breathe in through your nose. Take the breath deep into your body, breathe out through your mouth, breathe in through your nose and out through your mouth, once more in through the nose and out through the mouth. Now still concentrating on your breathing begin to breathe naturally......

You are sitting in your garden under the shade of an apple tree. It is a warm mid-August day; the sun is shining from a cloudless sky. You decide to go for a walk on this beautiful summer day, get up from your seat and walk to the garden gate. Open the gate and turn to your left, walk along the pavement until you reach a kissing gate on your left......Now walk along a farm track, the track is dry, the parched earth is red/brown. As you walk along the track there is a small wood to your left bordered by a sheep fence. To your right is a field of golden oats, the ears of the oats are rippling in a gentle breeze, the edge of the field is covered in bright red field poppies. In the distance you can see the romantic ruins of a sandstone castle. Continue to walk along the track heading towards the castle. The field of oats stretches way into the distance and that is bordered by yet more fields of golden wheat and barley...... As you look towards the distant fields you can see that the sky is turning a dark grey with a real threat of rain……. Sure enough you can hear the rumble of thunder in the distance and then a flash of lightening pierces the blackened sky. As you continue to walk along the track large spots of rain begin to fall, the ground is so hot and dry the raindrops dry immediately they touch the earth…...Suddenly without warning the heavens open and it pours with rain. Further along the track towards the castle is the tumbled down remains of the castle custodian's kiosk, run towards it…...Go inside the shack, despite there being no doors or windows the corrugated iron roof in still intact and provides shelter from the storm. Stand and watch the lightning, which is now lighting up the sky almost continuously, the thunder is crashing overhead. The rain drums down upon the roof of the shack……. Despite the ferocity of the storm you have no fear, instead you feel energised, vital and alive and relish the sounds of the rain and the storm……

In the distance you can see that the sky is becoming lighter. Now, as suddenly as it began, the rain stops, as you look up at the grey sky you can see a patch of blue is slowly appearing. The sun pierces the cloud sending down golden shafts of light. The heads of the oats are bowed down with the weight of the rain, as you watch the fields of oats, wheat, and barley steam in the warmth of the sun and slowly begin to raise their heavy heads…...The whole landscape is transformed into a magical, ethereal space and the golden fields almost seem to float amongst the heat haze. leave the shack and head for home back along the track taking care to avoid the puddles in the ruts left by the tractor wheels…...As you pass the trees they are also steaming in the heat, and you catch a glimpse of a roe deer as it shelters under the trees. You have reached the kissing gate, go through the gate, and turn left along the pavement, back towards your garden gate. Open the gate and go back to the apple tree in the garden…...

When you are ready to return slowly begin count down from

five, move your shoulders and head from side to side as you come back to the room. If you lit a candle when you blow it out send love and healing to those in need and take a moment to reflect upon the season. Take some small sips of water to ground yourself.

BLUE CHEESE AND PEAR SALAD SERVES 2

200g blue cheese, use a vegan version. If you can't get blue cheese this works well with vegan "Feta"
1 ripe pear, washed
50g walnuts
Lettuce, washed
Tomatoes
Cucumber

Cut the cheese into cubes. Crush the walnuts. Cut the pear lengthways, a large pear cuts into about 16 pieces. Pile the lettuce onto two plates now sprinkle half of the cheese and walnuts over the lettuce on each plate. Fan the pear around the edge. Add your chopped tomatoes and cucumber. Spoon over some salad dressing and enjoy with crusty bread and a glass of wine.

BREAD RECIPE

500g strong bread flour of your choice. I often use half white and half wholemeal or seeded
1 sachet fast acting bread yeast
Salt
2 tablespoons vegetable oil
1 teaspoon sugar
300ml warm water

Place all your dry ingredients into a bowl. Add the oil and water, don't make the water too hot you will kill the yeast. Using your hands mix to a smooth dough and knead for at least 10 minutes. Place into an oiled bowl and cover. Leave in a warm place for at least an hour until it has doubled in size. When the dough has risen knead again for 5 minutes and then shape and proove for 30 minutes then place into a preheated oven 200oC.

I use this dough for pizzas, fruit bread, olive bread, plaited bread the variations are endless. I find that a third of the dough is enough for a large pizza for two so I use the remaining dough to make rolls or a loaf. If I am making a fruit loaf I incorporate the fruit at the second kneading, likewise olives.

Enjoy experimenting.

BLACKBERRY WINE RECIPE

1500g (3lbs) Blackberries
1500g (3lbs) granulated sugar
1 heaped teaspoon pectolase
1 heaped teaspoon general purpose wine yeast
1heaped teaspoon yeast nutrient
1 camden tablet
6 pints boiling water

2 demijohns, airlocks, and corks
Muslin square
Plastic jug and funnel
Sterilising powder
1 metre clear plastic wine tubing

Large clean container with a lid that will hold at least 1 gallon of liquid

Pick your own blackberries. Pick over and clean your blackberries and remove any small insects and spiders which may be lurking amongst the fruit. Place your fruit in your clean lidded container and add the boiling water, usually two kettles full. Add the sugar and stir well until the sugar has fully dissolved.

Place the lid on the container. Ensure the lid fits well, if not weigh down with a heavy book. It is important that any wine flies (fruit flies) do not get into your wine at any stage, or the wine will spoil.

Leave to cool right down and then add 1 camden tablet and 1 teaspoon of pectolase. Stir well. Leave for 24 hours. Now add the yeast and yeast nutrient stir well and cover and leave in a warm kitchen for seven days. Keep an eye on the wine if the lid shows signs of lifting because of too much pressure build up you will need to vent it. Or BANG!

Following the instructions on the pack make up enough sterilising solution to clean one demijohn and your muslin square, jug, and funnel.

Carefully strain your wine must into your demijohn. When all the wine is in the demijohn add your airlock. Ensure that you place a water trap inside the airlock to prevent fruit flies from getting down into the wine and spoiling it. You may need to top up or replace your water during the fermentation process. I find several flies often get trapped inside.

Leave the wine in a warm place to "Work" for as long as it takes, probably at least two months. If you are unsure if the wine has finished working add a teaspoon of white sugar to the must, if the wine fizzes it hasn't finished working.

When the wine has finished, sterilise your second demijohn, tubing and cork. Remove the airlock and cork and using the tubing decant your wine into the clean demijohn. I find this works best if the clean demijohn is on the floor and the wine demijohn is on the worktop. Fit your cork and then store the wine before drinking. I usually store mine for around twelve months, but if you can't wait, four to six months should be ample. This should make six bottles of wine. When it comes to bottling, sterilise your bottles and tubing and then decant the wine into your bottles. Again, I usually have the bottles on the floor and the wine on the worktop.

Happy brewing. You can use any fruit or vegetable that you choose to make wine. We prefer the blackberry as mostly it tastes like port when it is ready to drink.

A VILLAGE TALE

SECOND HARVEST

O ur second harvest is now safely gathered in. Apples in the stores and honey in the jars, mead to make. Soon cheeses of cider apples will be piled high, golden juice running to fill the barrels. The Goddess has given the fruits of the hedgerows, vines, and orchards. Many blessings she bestows upon us. We give thanks to our Mother Gaia for all her bounty. Blessed Be!

Oak climbed up onto the large slab of rock in the orchard, all eyes turned towards him.

"Our apple harvest is now done for another year. Another year that we shall celebrate the safe gathering in of the fruits of nature, thank you for all your hard work today. Everyone has laboured from sunrise to sunset as is the custom. Now see, the sun is beginning to set, tomorrow we shall give thanks for our harvest."

Everyone cheered, sore arms, hands and backs forgotten. Everyone in the village always looked forward to the late harvest celebration feast. The weather was still warm and although the days were becoming noticeably shorter, winter was still a good while away.

Soon everyone had gone home and only Oak was left in the orchard. He sat quietly under the trees as the darkness of the night gathered around him. A vixen passed by, she was used to seeing Oak out and about in the orchard and woodlands and fields around the village, so paid him no heed. In the distance owls screeched and called, then, just as Oak was about to make for home an owl glided past on silent wings as it hunted for small mice and voles in the long grass at the edge of the orchard.

As Oak opened the front door of the cottage he had shared with his parents, Demi and Fin since birth, the wonderful aroma of baking cakes and pies greeted him. "That smells good, I'm going to miss this when you have left the village."

"Well for a start, you know perfectly well how to cook and bake, I have seen to that, and I shall be bringing cakes and pies for the feasts even after we have left the village," replied Demi smiling. Demi knew that Oak was finding it hard to adjust to the thought that Fin and Demi were leaving the village in a few short weeks at Samhain. Oak had known, since childhood, that this time would come, he also knew that he was more than ready to fulfil his role as Lord of the Wildwood and Lord of the Wildhunt. He knew deep down, that within a few days of Demi and Fin leaving, he would settle to running the house as he wanted and in some ways, he was looking forward to rearranging the furniture and kitchen how he would like it…..but it was a big change not only for Oak but for the whole village.

"Right, I am off to bed, I have to be up early to bake bread for tomorrow," said Demi yawning.

"I will join you," agreed Fin. "See you tomorrow for the ceremonies and feast," Fin continued. "Ceremonies? I can't think what you mean," said Oak playfully.

"Surely you can't possibly have forgotten it is the baby naming tomorrow for Willow, Hazel, and Raven's daughter?" Oak laughed. "No, I hadn't forgotten, how could I? All Raven did today was complain how tired he was as Willow had kept them awake most of the night. You won't catch me having babies for a long time yet."

Demi and Fin smiled, "You just wait, as soon as you are Handfasted to the right girl that will be all she will be wanting," said Fin.

"Well, I didn't, I wanted us to grow together as a couple and to learn as much as I could about the Village and customs before we had Oak. Not all girls are the same. You enjoy your freedom for a few years yet, my lad," said Demi.

"Oh, so that's it. A burden. A tie that's all I ever was," said Oak laughing.

"Oh, off to bed with you!" laughed Demi.

The next morning dawned bright and clear with that early morning chill in the air that warned of colder late autumn days to come. When Demi, Fin and Oak arrived at the orchard it was a hive of activity. The Altar had been set up ready for Fin and Oak to cover with the heavy cloth that had been embroidered with the symbols of the four elements around the edges and in the centre an apple tree heavily laden with fruit to signify the Spirit of Place.

Trestle tables had been set up around the edges of the orchard where food was being laid out ready for the harvest and baby naming feast. In the centre, in pride of place, were some beautifully iced cakes that Demi had made for the celebrations. When Fin and Demi left the village Demi planned to restart her cake baking and catering business.

When all was ready everyone began to assemble around the Altar. Hazel and Raven with baby Willow stood in the centre of the circle with Fin, Demi and Oak. Demi noticed that despite Raven's protestations that Willow never slept she was now sound asleep in Hazels arms.

Oak raised his hands and staff to signal that the ceremonies were about to begin.

"Welcome everyone. Welcome to our second harvest ceremony. Welcome to the naming ceremony of Hazel and Raven's daughter." Everyone smiled and clapped, "Steady now. Let sleeping babies lie," said Oak. Everyone laughed, the whole village had heard Raven complaining of his lack of sleep.

"Let us now welcome the Guardians of the Air, Fire, Water and Earth and give thanks to the Spirit of this beautiful place that we are fortunate to call home." The Guardians were called and the Spirit. The trees were thanked for their bounty and the Goddess thanked for the abundance of the harvest. "Now we come to the naming ceremony," began Oak, "Every family has been asked to bring an apple and a knife. During the ceremony I shall ask for the apple to be cut in half crosswise. Does everyone have an apple and a knife?" every family nodded. "Good. Now to begin." Oak walked to where Hazel and Raven stood, Hazel passed the sleeping child to Oak. "What do you name this child?"

"We name her Willow Rose," replied Hazel and Raven. Oak, Hazel, and Raven walked to the eastern quarter of the circle.

"Guardians of the East, Sprit of Air. We introduce you to Willow Rose, may she always have pure clear air to breathe. May only gentle winds and breezes fill the days of her life. Blessed Be." *"Blessed Be."*

Oak led the group to the southern quarter. "Guardians of the South. Spirit of Fire. We introduce you to Willow Rose, may her days be filled with warmth. May she never be cold or alone. Blessed Be" *"Blessed Be"*

Now they walked to the western quarter. "Guardians of the West. Spirit of Water. We introduce you to Willow Rose, may she always have pure clean, clear water to drink to sustain her all the days of her life. Blessed Be."

"Blessed Be."

The small group made their way to the northern quarter of the circle. "Guardians of the North. Spirit of Earth. We introduce you to Willow Rose, may she always have enough food to sustain her. May she never know hunger. May she treat our Mother Earth with reverence and respect. Blessed Be." *"Blessed Be."*

Finally, the small group returned to the centre of the circle. "Guardians of the Spirit of Place. We introduce you to Willow Rose, know this child as one of our great family. The family of this place we call home. Look and watch over her for all her days. Blessed Be."

"*Blessed Be.*"

Oak held the still sleeping child for all to see. "Welcome Willow Rose. Now everyone, please cut your apple cross wise to reveal the five quarters," the apples were cut and any pips that remained whole were saved to sow in the hope that some of them would germinate to raise a new generation of trees. "Now share the apple amongst your family, give thanks for our harvest and give thanks for this new child, this new life." The apples were shared and eaten, a small amount from each apple was placed upon the ground as an offering to the Earth Mother to give thanks for her bounty.

"Now it is time to enjoy our feast in the autumn sunshine. Time to cut the wonderful naming cakes. Enjoy the rest of your day."

SECOND HARVEST BOUNTY

Mountain Ash, Sorbus, Rowan, call it what you will,
Berries of yellow, orange, or red,
Food for foraging birds,
Sparkle brightly in the Indian Summer Sun.

Hazel and beech trees nuts abound.
Squirrels chase to harvest the pre-winter bounty,
Sweet chestnuts fall,
We harvest them to roast upon our open fires.

Horse Chestnuts glisten,
Rich brown skins within creamy white prickly cases,
Children and adults alike,
Gather them for Autumn fun and games.

Acorns fall.
Their tiny fairy cups fill a child's imagination,
With wide eyed awe they search,
For tiny doors at the base of the great woodland Oaks.

Rosehips, sloes and blackberries fill the hedgerows,
Soothing syrups, wines, and gins to prepare,
Winter chills to sooth and repel,
All are safely stored away.

Apples, plums, and pears we harvest,
Ladders propped precariously at the base of trees,
Apples to store, pears, and plums into jams we make,
Or to eat from the trees, juicy and sweet.

Onions, garlic, beans, and marrows now all gathered in,
Some we shall store,
Others will make tasty chutneys and pickles,
Our festive tables to grace.

Days and nights now of equal length,
We give our heartfelt thanks,
Our Goddess shares her Autumn Horn of Plenty,
Before Winter chills begin to bite.

MABON

The season of mellow fruitfulness is upon us,
The Goddess is in full bloom,
Ready for our second harvest.

Acorns, Hazel, and Beech nuts abound,
Horse Chestnuts fall,
See children having fun as they seek the shiny conkers.

Sweet chestnuts too are collected now, ready for a roasting
at Yule.
Hedgerows laden with Blackberries and sloe.
Gins, wines, and syrups all waiting to be made.

Trees droop from the weight of apples,
They begin to fall one by one.
Pies, crumbles, and apple cakes to bake.

Jams and chutneys bubble on the stove.
Larders to be laden ready for the long harsh winter months
ahead.
In the barns, cheeses of apples are pressed.

Early morning mists disappear as the sun begins to rise.
Hedges laden with dew glisten like diamonds as they sparkle
in sunlight.
Spider's webs invisible until now drape the hedgerows and
gardens in their thousands.

Long autumn walks kicking leaves as they crunch and crumble underfoot.

The breeze rattles the trees, we are showered with nuts and acorns.

We let out the occasional yelp as horse chestnuts fall onto unsuspecting heads.

Mellow Autumn days,

Truly a time to rejoice in all the bounty that nature has to offer,

We are Brightly Blessed.

ACORN MEDITATION

S it quietly where you won't be disturbed, take a drink to ground yourself when you return. Light a candle or some incense if appropriate, adjust your clothes and get comfortable......

Close your eyes and begin to relax......

When you are ready to begin concentrate on your breathing. Take in a deep breath, breathe in through your nose, take the breath deep into your body. Breathe out through your mouth, breathe in through your nose and out through your mouth, once more in through the nose and out through the mouth. Now still concentrating on your breathing begin to breathe naturally......

Imagine that you are in great wood of Oak trees, the ancient trees are covered in thick velvety green mosses and soft green lichens. The ancient boughs and branches reach for the clear blue sky of late Autumn......On the branches of the Oak trees are many large ripe acorns. Imagine that you are one of those acorns on the edge of one of the branches, you sway from side to side in the gentle breeze......As the breeze moves your branch you are dislodged and you fall slowly, silently to the earth......Some of the woodland deer were grazing under your tree during the night and left hoof prints in the soft spongy earth, you fall into one of the divots. The earth is cool and moist. As you lie there looking up through the branches of the tree, you can see the blue of the sky then, as the hours pass, the sky changes into the inky black of the night sky...... After a few days you are covered by fallen leaves, you are now safe and warm and protected from foraging animals looking for winter food. You are protected from the harsh winter winds and heavy snowfalls......

You are woken from your winter slumbers by the woodland birds beginning to sing. You see the blue sky once more; you now have tiny roots fixed firmly in the ground. Stretch and small green shoots pop up through the leaf cover and out of the ground. Stretch ever higher towards the light and the sky, stretch ever upwards enjoying the Spring sunshine on your new leaves, feel the warm soft gentle rains and feel gentle summer breezes......By Autumn you have grown, now as the wheel continues to turn, you are beginning to lose your leaves and settling down for your winter slumber......

When you are ready to return slowly begin count down from five. Move your shoulders and head from side to side as you come back to the room. If you lit a candle when you blow it out send love and healing to those in need and take a moment to reflect upon the elements. Take some small sips of water to ground yourself.

MUSHROOM ROLL

1 pack shop bought ready rolled puff pastry
I medium carrot, grated
1 onion, chopped
3 cloves garlic, crushed and chopped
Generous handful of fresh sage, chopped, or a dessertspoon dried sage
1 heaped teaspoon of yeast extract
1 dessertspoon soy sauce
1 level dessertspoon gravy granules, check suitable for vegans, or use cornflour
1 level dessertspoon yeast flakes
Glug of sweet sherry
400g can green lentils, drained and rinsed
150g button mushrooms or chestnut mushrooms chopped
Vegetable oil to fry
Ground black pepper to taste

Lightly fry the onions and garlic until soft but not brown. Add mushrooms cook for a few minutes until softened.

Add the sherry, yeast extract, soy sauce, and gravy granules, the sauce should thicken very quickly. If too thick add a little water. Don't make it too runny as it will escape from the pastry. Remove from heat. Let the mix cool slightly. Add the lentils, sage, yeast flakes and black pepper. I never use salt as the yeast extract and gravy granules are quite salty.

When cool spread the mix over half of the pastry leaving a gap of ½ inch. Moisten the pastry with water and fold over the top half of the pastry, seal by crimping the edges. Score the top of the pastry to allow steam to escape.

Cook 180oC for about 40 minutes.
This is lovely for a celebration dinner.

APPLE CAKE

125g Vegan Margarine

*1 mug of dried fruit of your choice

1 mug of granulated sugar, or half white and half brown sugar

1 mug of hot water

1 mug of chopped apples

2 mugs of self-raising flour or you can use plain flour and add 2 teaspoons of raising agent

1-2 teaspoons of spices of your choice, mixed spice, ginger, cinnamon etc

1 teaspoon of white wine vinegar

1 tablespoon of chia seeds

Grease and line two sponge tins or one loaf tin.

Set the oven for 160oC

Boil the kettle.

Place the margarine into a bowl and melt in the microwave for about 40 seconds

Add the dried fruit and sugar plus hot (not boiling) water. Stir well.

Whilst this is soaking peel and chop your apples. I usually find one large cooking apple is about one mug full.

Add the apple to your mixing bowl. Stir well.

Now add the rest of the ingredients, add the flour in stages otherwise it will become a very lumpy mix. Stir well.

Divide mix between the two sponge tins or place into your loaf tin.

The sponge tins size will cook in about 30-40 minutes the loaf tin about 50 minutes to an hour. Check it is cooked by probing with a skewer.

Place on a cooling rack and enjoy when cool. Freezes well.

If you are not a vegan instead of the chia seeds and vinegar, use one or two beaten eggs. DO NOT add the egg to a hot mix otherwise it will scramble!

1 use a 300ml mug.

PICKLED RED CABBAGE

1 large red cabbage

Salt

Spices of your choice (ginger, coriander, mustard seeds etc)

Mix of malt and white vinegar or you can use pickling vinegar which is already spiced.

Several jars, sterilised.

Finely chop your cabbage. Layer it into a large bowl, I usually use about a level dessert spoon of salt between each layer. I find a large cabbage will do around three or four layers. Cover the cabbage and salt mix and place in the fridge for 24 hours. Now give your cabbage mix a good wash to remove the salt residue. Dry the cabbage in batches between kitchen paper.

Stuff the cabbage into the sterilised jars. Really press it down hard. Cover your cabbage with the vinegar. If you are not using ready spiced vinegar add your spices. I usually use about half a teaspoon of spice per jar.

Put the lids on your jars and store in a dark cupboard for at least a month before eating. Keeps well for at least three months.

TOMATO CHUTNEY

950g tomatoes. (I use either green or red tomatoes for this recipe)
500g chopped apples
250g brown sugar
375g sultanas
1 large onion
1 heaped tablespoon mixed spice
1 pint vinegar, I usually use malt
Salt to taste
Sterilised jars

Skin and chop the tomatoes. The easiest way to do this is to pierce the skin and place them in a bowl with some boiling water for about 15 minutes. Add the tomatoes to the rest of the ingredients in a very large pan and bring slowly to the boil stirring occasionally. Simmer for at least two hours until the mix has thickened and turned a lovely dark colour. Pour into your jars and seal. Keeps about four months.

Phil tells me that this is amazing and that he loves either version, but the red tomato chutney is slightly better. I don't like chutney I only make it for him.

BLACKBERRY VODKA

300g washed blackberries
300g granulated sugar
1 litre vodka
1 empty one litre bottle

Divide the vodka between the two bottles using a funnel, add 150g sugar to each bottle plus 150g blackberries.

Ensure the lids are on both bottles and shake them until the sugar has dissolved. Shake the bottles several times over the next 24 hours then put them away for about two months, by then it should be ready to drink.

Enjoy it on its own or as part of a cocktail. It's also lovely drizzled over vanilla ice cream. The used berries also have a kick if you add a few to ice cream.

If you find this a little sweet, reduce the amount of sugar.

This is the basic recipe. You can use the same recipe using raspberries or blackcurrants. The vodka can be substituted for gin, and you can make fruit gins using the same method.

SAMHAIN

A VILLAGE TALE

The Wheel continues to turn, seasons come, and seasons go. Nature in all her guises as Maiden, Mother and Crone. We are all born, we live, and we eventually die, that is the way of the Wheel, that is the way of life. All things must pass to make way for new generations.

Demi was sitting on the large flat boulder in the middle of the stream in the Glade, her knees were drawn up towards her chin and her arms were wrapped tightly around her legs. It was very cold as the sun didn't penetrate the Glade until much later in the day at this time of the year. The holly trees were already covered in shiny, bright red berries and the blackbirds were gorging themselves. Above the Crows and Ravens were beginning to assemble ready for the ceremony tomorrow, this would be the last ceremony that Demi and Fin would lead as Lady of the Land and Harvest and Lord of the Wildhunt. Tomorrow evening Demi and Fin would lead the souls of the recently departed across the Bridge from the village for the first and last time. They would leave their beloved son Oak at the boundary of the village because if he left the village after sunset he would begin to age as a mortal and lose his powers as the Lord of the Wildwood and Lord of the Wildhunt. Tomorrow Fin and Demi would walk out of the village to lead the way. The Crows and Ravens would then accompany the Souls whilst Fin and Demi headed for their cottage in the hamlet over in the next valley. This would now be their home for however long their lives would last, for Demi and Fin would now become as mortals and begin to age and grow old together.

"I thought that I would find you here," Demi started, she had been so engrossed in her thoughts that she hadn't heard Fin approaching.

"It is where we first met, it is where Oak was conceived and where I was also conceived, it is my special place."

"Yes, it is very special, don't forget we can visit whenever you want us to. It is a special place, the place of the Fae, where we danced on Midsummer's Eve all those years ago. It is as though it was just yesterday."

Demi smiled, "Well it does almost seem that way, so much has happened. Our handfasting, Oak's birth, losing Sweetbriar and Beech and my parents too. All the ceremonies we have led, all the learning and growing up I had to do." Fin helped Demi to her feet and held her in his arms, he too was feeling a great sadness to be leaving the village that had been his home for many generations. He looked into Demi's eyes and could see that the tears were beginning to form.

"Now don't cry fair Lady. This was planned, we knew that this day would come, the day that Oak was born, we knew that when he was twenty-four, we would leave the Village. It will be a wrench for the lad too."

Demi smiled through her tears, "Yes, it is time, I am in a way, looking forward to exploring the outside world once more. Looking forward to staying away from home for a few nights occasionally. Looking forward to starting up my cake baking and catering business, after all we shall need to support ourselves financially now." Fin laughed.

"It sounds as though you have thought things through. Yes, I agree, I can do some painting and decorating and odd jobs to help swell the coffers. We shall manage well; we don't need much."

"Just each other," whispered Demi.

"Yes just each other," agreed Fin. "Come on let's have a walk through the woods and up to the top fields to our favourite 'leaning on the gate place.'" Laughing they left the

Glade arm in arm.

In his turn Oak was sitting quietly in the orchard, soon it would be time to set up the Altar to prepare for the ceremony for tomorrow. He was feeling very much alone, yet elated and afraid of the future in equal proportions. He had never lived alone; his parents had always been there to provide support and help and advice when he needed it. Yes, he was used to being alone, many times he had spent hours walking in the fields and woodlands and he had spent many nights alone wandering the woodlands watching the over the local wildlife......but this was going to be a different alone.

"Hey, come on sleepyhead, stop slouching around and help set up the Altar ready for tomorrow!" Raven's voice bought Oak back to the present with a rush. Of course, Oak wouldn't be alone. Demi and Fin would be just over in the next valley, he had friends aplenty and everyone in the village knew and loved him. He would be fine, Oak mentally scolded himself, stop feeling sorry for yourself life will go on and you are more than ready for the challenge, "On my way!"

Samhain dawned cold and bright, there was a distinct promise of the colder, darker days to come. As ever, Demi had been up and about early baking bread and cakes for the feast that evening. She kept telling herself that this would not be the last time she would be doing this, as even after they had left the village Demi and Fin would be returning for the ceremonies. However, deep down Demi knew that those times would become less and less as they had planned to let Oak lead the ceremonies the way he thought fit and to bring about subtle changes to ensure that the village kept abreast with modern changes, ideas, and technology.

"That smells good," Fin entered the kitchen a smile on his face, it was a forced smile as, like Demi, he was struggling to come to terms with leaving their home in the village and making the family cottage in the next valley their new home. Fin had spent several weeks redecorating and ensuring that all repairs had been carried out prior to the winter. Demi had made new curtains and throws, and the cottage now had a homely cosy feel to it that it hadn't had when Sweetbriar and Beech had lived there. Yes, times are changing, we have made changes to our future home as Oak will make changes to this cottage when we have left it, life goes on as usual and yet it changes too. Fin thought to himself.

The front door opened, and Oak appeared in the kitchen sniffing the air, "Mmm, you have been busy."

"Is everything set for later, do we need to set out the tables in the village hall ready for the feast?"

"No all is done. Everything is ready, the hall is ready, and we have made the finishing touches to the bonfire," Oak's voice choked as he continued, "It's shame that you won't be eating some of those delicious smelling cakes."

Demi gave Oak a hug, "All will be well. You will do a fantastic job. The ceremony tonight will be the best Samhain ceremony for many years. You will do our Ancestors and the newly departed Souls proud."

Fin lightened the mood with, "Who is ready for lunch?"

As night began to fall everyone began to assemble in the orchard and to form a circle, those who had lost a dear one since last Samhain joined Demi, Fin, and Oak in the centre of the circle.

Oak raised his staff in the air and silence fell over the orchard.

"Tonight, we give thanks for the Ancestors, and we bid a final farewell to those who have passed while the Wheel has turned since our last Samhain ceremony. This year, as the Souls leave the Village on their final journey, they will be accompanied part of the way by Demi and Fin. They will lead the Souls towards the Bridge and the Ravens and Crows will in turn lead them on to the Summerlands over the Bridge to their new home. Let us welcome and give thanks to the Guardians of the elements who have nourished and sustained the lives of those who we have loved."

The Guardians were called and thanked in turn. The cords were cut to release the Souls from their binding to the earth. Now Oak raised his staff into the air once more for quiet.

"Lastly, we say farewell to Demi and Fin who have worked tirelessly for many generations to ensure that everyone in the Village has been well cared for. They have cared for the woodlands and the gardens; they have ensured that no one has ever gone hungry or been cold during the winter months." The orchard erupted into a wall of noise as everyone wanted to express their thanks to Demi and Fin for everything that they had done over the years.

Fin stepped forward, "Thank you everyone for the good wishes that Demi and I have received over the past few weeks since we decided to leave the Village in Oaks's capable hands. We shall both miss you as much as you will miss us. Fear not we shall be returning for the festivals and ceremonies."

Demi stepped forward, "It is many years since I moved to this wonderful village, I had a great deal of growing up to do and I had to learn a great deal too. I can only express my thanks and gratitude to everyone who helped me in those first few months and years. I also know that if Oak needs any guidance someone will be willing to help him. Thank you one and all."

Fin came to stand next to Demi, "It is time for us to leave, it is time for us to make our first nighttime journey out of the village as we lead the Souls who are patiently waiting, towards the Bridge. We leave now with heavy hearts."

Fin and Demi picked up the packs that held their last few belongings and hand in hand made their way out of the circle and up the hill towards the boundary of the Village towards the area where the Souls would leave escorted by the Ravens and Crows.

As Demi and Fin reached the top of the village they stopped for a while leaning on 'Their' gate, the gate that they had leant upon all those years ago when they had first celebrated the Summer Solstice and Demi had danced the night away in the Glade.

"The Village will be fine, Oak will care for it as lovingly as we have done over the years, come now my love, it is our turn to celebrate the rest of our lives together," with a final glance over their shoulders Demi and Fin began the climb over the hill into the next valley and their new home.

After Fin and Demi had left the circle, everyone began to drift away towards the village hall where the Samhain feast was laid out. Oak, for once, was not feeling hungry. He sat alone in the orchard imagining Fin and Demi's journey in his mind. At last, when he was sure that they had made it safely to their new home he began to walk slowly towards the hall and village green. As Oak neared the green, he could hear laughter and the splashing of water, the apple bobbing was in progress. Just as he approached someone placed a lighted stick into his hand.

"Come on light the Samhain bonfire." Oak thrust the burning brand into the centre of the bonfire and almost immediately the night sky was lit by the red and orange flames. Oak felt a hand on his shoulder.

"Come on, you could do with some food and a jar or two of cider," Oak turned, and Raven propelled Oak towards the hall where he placed a plate laden with food and a glass brimming with cider into Oaks hands. Raven led Oak towards a table, "There is someone I would like you to meet, it is my cousin, she has just moved into the area."

"Hi, you must be Oak, Raven has told me so much about you. My name is Gai, well it's Gaia really but my friends call me Gai."

SAMHAIN GLORY

The Wheel has turned from Samain to Samhain,
The time for thoughts and reflections is here,
To remember those dear ones who have recently passed,
Those whom we knew and loved in more distant times.

Coppery coloured Beech leaves drift silently to the ground,
Field Maple, multi-coloured leaves of yellow, gold, and red,
Crisp dry leaves underfoot, we kick and crunch them as we
walk,
Patterns of copper, yellow, red and brown adorn the lawns
and fields alike.

The veil between worlds is at its thinnest,
With fond memories we invite back into our lives those we
have lost, the moment will be brief,
As we cycle down into the dark days of winter, keep light, and
hope in your hearts,
Soon we shall be celebrating the rebirth of the Sun God at
Yule.

Shafts of sunlight pierce the branches that lift naked limbs
towards the sky,
Children squeal with delight as they gather armfuls of leaves,
skywards to throw,
Shrieks of laughter ring out as they rain down upon them
once more,
Toadstools peek from the leaf litter so deep, colours of late
Autumn against the bronzed leaves.

The Crone sits patiently awaiting the new God,
For now, rest and reflect, begin making your own plans for
the future,
Tell tales and store food and drink against the harsh winter
months,
Spend precious time with those who we love.

SAMHAIN MEDITATION

Sit quietly where you won't be disturbed, take a drink to ground yourself when you return. Light a candle or some incense if appropriate, adjust your clothes and get comfortable......

Close your eyes and begin to relax......

When you are ready to begin concentrate on your breathing. Take in a deep breath, breathe in through your nose, take the breath deep into your body, breathe out through your mouth. Breathe in through your nose and out through your mouth, once more in through the nose and out through the mouth. Now still concentrating on your breathing begin to breathe naturally......

You are sitting in a comfortable armchair near to a warm fire, it is dark in the room as all of the lights have been turned off. The curtains are open and outside the full moon is just beginning to rise in a clear starlit sky over open fields. Get up from your chair and walk to the hallway, put on your warmest coat, hat and gloves and pick up the torch next to the front door......Open the front door and walk across a small yard towards a gate into the field opposite, open the gate and go into the field. It is so light that you don't need your torch, put it into your coat pocket, and walk across the field to a circle of standing stones......In the distance an owl hoots and a vixen barks. All are natural sounds of the night. You have reached the entrance to the stone circle. Stand and look up at the great standing stones that tower above you......Enter the stone circle, do you feel anything, do you feel the energy from the stones? Walk towards one of the stones and place your hands on the surface of stone, feel the texture of the stone. Is it rough or is it smooth, is it covered in moss or lichen? Stand

at one with the stone, feel the energy from the stone......
The moon has risen higher, it's bright light illuminating the
plain beyond the stone circle. Look up at the sky, look at the
stars. Hundreds and hundreds of stars they look so close
that you could almost reach up and touch them. Planets and
constellations, Mars, Venus, Orion, Ursa Major......There is
a stone row to your right, walk towards the stone row.......
The stones tower above you, you see that there is a pathway
between the two rows of stones walk towards it. Begin to
walk along the pathway down a gentle slope until you reach a
kissing gate......Go through the gate and begin to walk up a
slight incline towards the long barrow at the top of the hill.......
Something catches your eye, two hares have been disturbed,
they run across the field away from you towards a stand of
trees in the distance. Watch them until they disappear.......
Now continue your way up the hill to the barrow.......You
reach the barrow. Outside of the barrow are three giant
stones guarding the entrance. Place your hand on the nearest
stone, it feels smooth and cool. Do you feel the energy of this
place? Take the torch from your pocket and enter the barrow,
there is a passage in front of you. To each side of the passage
are several small chambers. Make your way to the end of the
passage, turn around and with your back to the stone look
back towards the entrance of the barrow. The moonlight is
streaming into the passage, stand as the ancestors used to do.
Think of those who have gone before, of the ancestors who
built this monument, think of your family ancestors both
ancient and recent. Do you feel the energy of this sacred space,
stay here for a short while.......Now as you leave the barrow,
give thanks for this sacred space. Outside the moonlight is so
bright it almost hurts your eyes, turn to your right, and climb
the small flight of steps onto the top of the barrow. Feel the
energy rise from the barrow, up through your feet and up
your legs, into your back and up to your shoulders and arms
and finally to the very top of your head. Stand and absorb the

energy…....When you are ready begin to walk back down the slope to the kissing gate…....Go through the gate and walk back up the slope between the standing stones….... Walk back through the stone circle and across the field to the gate…..... Walk through the gate and cross the yard and enter the front door of your house. Remove your coat and shoes and return to your armchair.

When you are ready to return slowly begin count down from five, move your shoulders and head from side to side as you come back to the room. If you lit a candle when you blow it out send love and healing to those in need and take a moment to reflect upon the season. Take some small sips of water to ground yourself.

The inspiration for this meditation is Avebury Stone circle and West Kennet Long Barrow.

SPICY PUMPKIN SOUP

I devised this recipe to use up the inevitable leftovers after Pumpkin carving every Samhain. It works equally well with Butternut Squash.

500g pumpkin or butternut squash cut into small cubes
125g red lentils
1 onion chopped
3 cloves of garlic crushed and chopped
1 large carrot peeled and chopped
1 teaspoon ground ginger
1 teaspoon mild chilli powder
1 teaspoon paprika
ground black or white pepper
1 heaped dessert spoon yeast flakes
1 vegetable stock cube
1 tablespoon oil for frying

Fry the onions and garlic until softened but not brown. Add all the spices and stir for one minute to cook the spices and bring out the flavour. Add the squash, carrot and lentils and enough boiling water to just cover the vegetables. Simmer for about 15 minutes and then add the stock cube. At this point you may need to add a small amount of water if it has all been absorbed by the lentils. Simmer for a further 30 minutes or so. You can either blitz in a food processor or leave it as a chunky soup.

As I am using a stock cube, I never add any salt until I have tasted the soup.

Serve with crusty bread or cheese scones.

SPAGHETTI BOLOGNESE, SERVES 4

This is my vegan version of a classic that we have been making for many years.

1 onion chopped
1 large carrot grated
2 cloves garlic crushed and chopped
390g can of green or brown lentils, rinsed and drained OR 250g frozen vegan mince
8 large tomatoes skinned and chopped or use a jar of bought sauce. Check the label
1 heaped tablespoon tomato puree
1 level dessert spoon yeast extract
1 heaped dessert spoon yeast flakes
Dried or fresh Italian herbs, dessert spoon of dried herbs or a good handful of fresh herbs
Oil to fry
Water if the mix is a little dry
Black pepper
(½ teaspoon sugar if using fresh tomatoes)

Dry spaghetti

Fry the onion and garlic in a little oil until opaque. Add the skinned tomatoes (and sugar) or jar of sauce, carrot, tomato puree, yeast extract, lentils or vegan mince, herbs, and tomato puree. Simmer for 40 minutes. Add black pepper to taste and the yeast flakes, simmer for another 5 minutes. Serve with cooked spaghetti. This freezes well.

I never add extra salt as the yeast extract is quite salty

SAVOURY RICE AND VEGAN SAUSAGES, SERVES 4

1 large onion finely chopped
3 cloves garlic crushed and chopped
2 peppers deseeded and chopped into fine dice
1 small mug long grain white rice
100g peas, fresh or frozen
large handful of fresh spinach
Chopped sage leaves or dried herbs
1 vegetable stock cube
vegetable oil for frying
boiling water
pepper
salt

In a large saucepan fry the onion and garlic until opaque. Add the peppers fry for about 5 minutes don't let the peppers catch and burn. Add the rice, stock cube and two mugs boiling water. Cover and simmer for about 15 minutes. Now stir in the peas. Cover and simmer for 5 minutes. Stir in the spinach and herbs about 2 minutes before serving. Add pepper and salt if using.

In a separate pan cook the sausages as per pack instructions.

Pile the rice onto a warmed plates or dishes place a couple of sausages on top of each serving.

When they were growing up our kids loved this. It was great way to get them to eat fresh seasonal veg. If you use different coloured peppers, it looks really pretty.

POSTSCRIPT

It is dusk. It is a few days before Samhain. Two figures make their way slowly and painfully into the Glade. The sun has almost set, the sky is very clear with the promise of a starlit night, a full moon, and a bitterly cold hard frost.

The figures are that of a man and a woman, both are bent forward and leaning on sticks. The women links her hand through the man's arm for extra support.

Their breath hangs in the cold night air.

Slowly they progress, at last they reach their destination. The man helps the woman onto the flat stone in the centre of the Glade.

They lie down, even though the stone is covered in soft moss it is still bitterly cold, the chill leeches through their clothes.

They lie together once more in the Glade where they first met many lifetimes ago, or is it the most fleeting and shortest of times?

As they lie together wrapped in each other's arms they turn and face one another. Fin runs his hands through Demi's hair. The long grey locks have disappeared. Once more, for a fleeting time the long red tresses shine in the moonlight, her face is smooth and unlined.

In her turn Demi runs her hands through the curls of Fin's shoulder length brown hair, all trace of care lines erased from his face.

For the last time they lie together as lovers, under the starlit sky, the Goddess Moon bestowing her blessings.

The moment passes.

The new dawn breaks. Two Souls stand hand in hand looking down upon the shell of their former bodies. They await the Lord of the Wildhunt to lead them to their new lives beyond the Bridge.

ACKNOWLEDGEMENTS

As ever my thanks to Phil for all of his encouragement and to my friends, Eileen and Freda who nagged and suggested I write this book to complete Demi, Fin's and Oak's stories.

My sincere thanks to Jan for proof reading and making helpful suggestions. Thank you.

Also many thanks to Richard the vet for checking my accuracy of animal husbandry.

Thanks also to the Design Hive for the cover and typesetting and to Alexa at Compass publishing for all of her help and guidance.

Thanks too to all who read my first book, The Wheel of the Year, I hope that you have enjoyed this book too.

Also thank you to the village of Lustleigh and surrounding area for the inspiration and locations for most of my stories.

Last but not least, I give thanks to Our Mother, The Earth for all of her bounty. Blessed Be.

Printed in Great Britain
by Amazon